THE RIVER SINGERS

Praise for

THE RIVER SINGERS

'A hymn to nature, written with compassion and flair.'
Lauren St John, author of *The White Giraffe*

'Just the sort of book I would have loved to have picked up as a child. I love the way Tom weaves in the natural history of the riverbank with a fast paced adventure.'
Gill Lewis, author of *Sky Hawk*

'This book became one of my favourites. I was worried what Sylvan, his brothers and sisters would do next! There was a lot of danger in their long journey. I couldn't wait to turn over the next page because I was full of excitement.'
Momo, age 8

'The book was amazing—it was the best book that I have ever read. I felt like I was in the book. My eyes would just not stop reading. I will recommend it to lots of people.'
Lulu, age 9

'With echoes of *The Wind in the Willows* by Kenneth Grahame and *Watership Down* this is a wonderful story with a classic, traditional feel. The writing style is lovely and the descriptions vividly conjure up the animals' world on the riverbank. The setting in an English countryside, together with the absence of people and the modern world, give this book a timeless quality . . . An utterly lovely book and highly recommended.'
The Bookbag

OXFORD
UNIVERSITY PRESS

Great Clarendon Street, Oxford OX2 6DP

Oxford University Press is a department of the University of Oxford.
It furthers the University's objective of excellence in research, scholarship,
and education by publishing worldwide in

Oxford New York

Auckland Cape Town Dar es Salaam Hong Kong Karachi
Kuala Lumpur Madrid Melbourne Mexico City Nairobi
New Delhi Shanghai Taipei Toronto

With offices in
Argentina Austria Brazil Chile Czech Republic France Greece
Guatemala Hungary Italy Japan Poland Portugal Singapore
South Korea Switzerland Thailand Turkey Ukraine Vietnam

Text © Tom Moorhouse 2013
Artwork © Simon Mendez 2013

The moral rights of the author and illustrator have been asserted

Database right Oxford University Press (maker)

First published 2013

British Library Cataloguing in Publication Data available

ISBN: 978-0-19-273480-8

10 9 8 7 6 5 4 3 2 1

Printed and bound by CPI Group (UK) Ltd, Croydon, CR0 4YY

Paper used in the production of this book is a natural,
recyclable product made from wood grown in sustainable forests.
The manufacturing process conforms to the environmental
regulations of the country of origin.

THE RIVER SINGERS

Tom Moorhouse

Illustrated by Simon Mendez

OXFORD
UNIVERSITY PRESS

FOR ANGELIKI

PROLOGUE

The rumour spread from burrow to burrow down the length of the Great River. The females, eyeing each other over their boundaries, commented on it in hushed tones. The males spoke of it with raised chins and defiant looks, before moving on and away to their own business. The rumour told of a new danger to the Folk. It told of a horror which came in the night. It told of the Great River stripped bare of her people, of entire colonies gone. It told of the end of their world.

But perhaps, they thought, a rumour is all it was. The ancient enemies—the fox, heron, weasel—had always been there, awaiting the unwary or unlucky. And still the Folk prospered. The Great River sang, her grasses were plentiful, and her waters were warm and bustling with life. No, perhaps rumours were only rumours and the lives of the Folk would continue as before. But even so the mothers turned an eye to their young, and slept more lightly than they had. And the males scented the breeze more carefully before straying into the open, ran more quickly, fed more watchfully.

Sylvan and the others, nestling in their chamber, knew nothing of the rumours. They knew nothing of the outside. They knew their mother, the scents of their home, and the rhythms of the Great River. They knew hunger which could be quenched with milk. But one day they would learn that sometimes a rumour is more than a rumour. Sometimes a rumour is a life which has yet to come.

PART 1
THE GREAT RIVER

The dawn was grey and the waters quiet. Sylvan was the first awake, lying with his brother and sisters in a pile of cosily intertwined limbs. Their breathing lulled him even as lightness spread up the tunnel and into the chamber, bringing with it the scent of morning. He yawned. He opened his eyes. He grinned. Today was the day. At last.

Sylvan extracted himself, ignoring the others' sleepy protests, and sat with twitching whiskers at the entrance to the chamber. He should wait for them, he knew. They were supposed to go out all together. But the air stirred with a promise of new things and, with a final glance at his siblings, he stole away down the tunnel, paws padding on the soil. He had known the way for ages now. A left, a right, loop around a knot of roots, then pause at the place where the roof had fallen. One eye to the sky. Quiver. Listen. Check the scents. Then onwards and downwards to the lower places, the entrance to the Great River and the gateway to the world.

With each downward step the light grew brighter and the air fresher, more exhilarating. Another turn, a slight rise. And there she was: the Great River. Her waters, lapping against the family's trampled little platform, were bright through the shade of the tall grasses. She filled him with her vastness, her movement, her song. He felt the stirrings of hunger, the desire to dive, to twist, to flow with her. He hesitated, one forefoot raised, everything urging him out and into the world.

'And what exactly do you think you're doing, young vole?'

A paw was on his tail, pinning it to the floor.

Sylvan froze. He placed his foot hurriedly back onto the ground. As his mother removed her paw he turned, radiating guilt.

'Nothing.'

Her whiskers were stiff with disapproval. 'What have I told you about coming here?'

Sylvan dropped his gaze. 'I'm not allowed to. It's dangerous on my own,' he recited.

'That's right. So what are you doing?'

'Just looking.'

'Hmm. Well, that's just as well. Because any of my offspring stupid enough to think that he could go off exploring on his own would find himself in here gnawing nettle roots while the rest of us were outside. Understood, Sylvan?'

'Yes, Mother. Sorry.'

'I should think so.' She surveyed the dejected water vole in front of her. 'I tell you what: since it's a nice calm day, and seeing as I promised, I don't see why we can't still have that little trip out. Together.'

Sylvan's head came up. 'Really?'

'Really. Now why don't you go and wake the others?'

'Yes, Mother. It's—' He was almost dancing on the spot, torn between his desire to stay near the water and the rush to fetch his siblings.

She turned. 'What, dear?'

'It's wonderful,' he blurted.

She smiled, showing her strong, orange teeth. 'Yes, dear, it is. Now go.'

Sylvan scampered back to the nest where his brothers and sisters were still sleeping. He rushed into the chamber and pawed at the flank of the nearest.

'Come on, Fern. It's today.'

'G'way.' Her voice was muffled, cuddled up against her sister.

'But it's today.'

'Please go away.'

He clambered over the heap and shook at his brother's shoulder. 'Wake up. We're going out today.'

Orris opened his eyes. 'Out?'

'Yes, out.'

'Don't want to. Leave me alone.' Orris huddled in on himself.

Sylvan gave him a disgusted look and turned his attention to Aven's diminutive frame, giving her a brotherly kick on the haunch.

'Come on, Tiny. Mother's promised we're going out today.'

Aven gasped and sat upright, pawing the sleep from her eyes. She groomed a little, setting her fur straight. She blinked her black eyes into focus.

'Sylvan,' she said sweetly, 'if you ever call me that again I'll gnaw your ears off.'

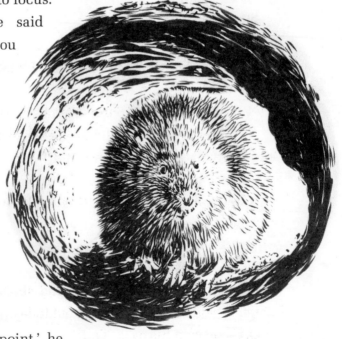

Sylvan grinned. 'You'll have to catch me first.'

'Or wait until you're asleep.'

He thought about it. 'Good point,' he conceded. 'Can we go out now?'

Orris uncurled a little. 'What's so good about going out, anyway?'

Sylvan sat back on his hind feet. 'I don't know. It's just . . . better out there.'

'Better?' said Orris. 'Only if "better" means "full of weasels and owls and things that want to eat us". I think I'll stay here.'

'Mother said we're going out,' said Sylvan, stubbornly.

'I hope you enjoy yourselves.'

'Look,' said Sylvan, 'I'm the oldest and you need to do what I say.'

'Says who?' said Aven.

Fern raised her head. 'Will you please all go away? I'm trying to sleep.'

'Well you shouldn't be. It's daytime,' said Sylvan.

'I—' began Fern, but the argument was cut short by the sound of their mother padding up the tunnel to the chamber. She bustled in and smiled at her family.

'Good morning, my dears,' she said. 'Are you all awake?'

'Yes. Unfortunately we are,' said Fern, giving Sylvan a dirty look.

'And are you ready to go out?'

'Yes,' said Sylvan before anyone else could respond.

Their mother surveyed them, approvingly. 'Good. Then I'll see you down at the entrance. Today's a big day. Today you're going to meet Sinethis.'

Sylvan scampered up and down between the nest and the entrance, herding and chivvying his siblings towards the water. Fern deliberately took her time just to annoy him. Orris was even more reluctant, complaining that he couldn't see the point in the outside and that the burrow was fine, wasn't it? Aven responded with unnecessary sarcasm, but looked almost as keen as Sylvan to get her first experience of the outside. She arrived at the entrance only a little after he did and they waited for the others with their noses poking out of the shade, revelling in the unfamiliar scents and sounds.

Sylvan glanced back up the tunnel. 'Come on, come on,' he muttered. His stomach rumbled.

'Hungry?' asked Aven.

'Yes, starving,' he said, surprised. In his excitement he almost hadn't noticed.

'Thought you might be. We haven't had any milk today.'

'That's true. I wonder why not?'

'I suppose Mother wanted us to go out first.'

Sylvan glared back up the tunnel. 'Right. That's it,' he said. 'They're between me and my food. I'm going to get them.'

He was about to set off when muffled scrabbling noises announced their arrival.

'Finally!' said Sylvan. 'Now all we need is Mother.'

Their mother had been out, scouting her territory, surveying for danger. She returned after a little while, ducking into the burrow. She stood in the entrance, placing herself between them and the outside. She looked down at her children: Sylvan and Aven expectant, Fern grumpy, and Orris nervous.

'So soon,' she said, almost to herself. She turned and stared out at the water and then back, with an odd expression.

'Well, young ones, beyond this point lies Sinethis, the Great River. We are River Singers, Water Folk, children of Sinethis. We live by her ways. She takes our old and gives us young. She stirs our hunger, feeds us with grasses. She shelters us in her waters and burrows. She rises and dashes us. She sings with us a song as soft as thistles, hard as roots, deep as shadows, old as stones. We sing with her a song as quick as thinking, sweet as apples, brief as day. We are River Singers, and we are hers.'

Sylvan had never heard these words before. None of them had.

When their mother finished, she nodded, once.

'These words I give you, which my mother gave to me. Learn them and live by them and perhaps you too will pass them to young of your own.'

Standing on the threshold, Sylvan felt oddly uneasy. Until now he had envisaged a joyful escape from the confines of the burrow into the glorious world beyond. But something in their mother's face, and the solemnity of her words, made him feel exposed and small.

'What if we don't go?' said Orris. They turned to him. 'I mean, who says that we have to? It's safe here. We could stay.'

'I know, dear.' Their mother's voice was soft. 'But you have no choice.'

'I do.' He looked abashed but defiant.

'Do you? Really? Remember what I said? "She stirs our hunger". Are you hungry, Orris?'

He nodded.

'And what would you like to eat?'

No reply.

'Milk?' she pressed.

Orris shook his head, reluctantly. Sylvan thought about it. He had never been so hungry, but milk, somehow, wouldn't do. Not any more.

'Come on. I'll show you the way,' said their mother.

She sniffed the air and with a patter of feet was gone. The

youngsters exchanged glances. Sylvan looked at his siblings and then back at the river. Despite his misgivings a fierce joy welled up in him. He grinned.

'Last one out's a rat.'

And he ran out into the dazzling daylight, almost colliding with his mother as she munched on a reed stem a little way beyond the burrow entrance.

He squeaked, 'Did I really do it? Am I really out?'

She put the stem down on the pile at her feet and smiled. 'Yes, dear,' she said. 'Now stay close and wait for the others.'

Sheltering grasses waved overhead, parting to reveal the patchy blue beyond. Scents mingled in the breeze: pollen, soil, water, and a thousand other, unfamiliar smells. The light was bright and the shadow deep. He ran to the water's edge. Here was their burrow marker, the bare mud platform covered with his mother's droppings and scent. He wrinkled his nose at the mixture of odours. Then he gazed down into the water. The river was clear right down to the lower, submerged burrow entrance, and to the plants on the bed. He touched the surface with his nose. Cold. Delicious.

'Sylvan.'

Reluctantly he obeyed the warning tone in her voice and joined her, now with the others a little way up the bank. They were arranged in a circle around a towering patch of sweet-grass stems, squinting in the brightness, sniffing at the air.

'So, here you are. Welcome, my loves, to the Great River. But be careful out here. Every moment you spend in the open you need to be alert. If you hear anything odd—anything at all—freeze, be silent. If things go wrong, run, make it to the water or to the burrow and you'll be safe.'

She smiled. 'Well. Lecture over. Now that you are finally too big for milk, you will have to eat like the rest of us. I think it's about time you learned to feed yourselves. Like this.'

She grasped a thick sweet-grass stem and with a deft bite severed it from the base. Holding it upright, she

ran it through her paws, expertly chopping it into lengths with her teeth, gnawing at the soft flesh and leaving aside the coarse outer parts. When she had finished there was a pile of discarded pieces at her feet.

'Go on,' she said. 'Try it.'

Sylvan grabbed for the largest stem he could find, making it shake far above him. Then he began chewing through the base. It was not easy. The outside was thick and dry, but the sweet juices from the middle flooded his mouth. He gnawed until his jaw ached, until only a few fibres held the giant plant upright, until . . . He realized his mistake only when the stem toppled sideways from his grasp and onto Fern's head.

'Ouch. Sylvan, will you please watch what you're doing?'

'Sorry.'

'You,' she said primly, 'are an idiot.' She turned back to her feeding. Sylvan wondered briefly about shoving her into the water. It probably wouldn't be a popular idea. Instead he abandoned his gigantic stem for a patch of smaller, new-grown woundworts. They tasted even better than the grass: less tough and a bit less bitter.

After a while they got the hang of things and grazed with peaceful industry. Even Orris relaxed, munching on greenery at the water's edge. The sun came out, making the deep shade of the bank more cool and welcoming. The only noises were the burble of the water, the calls of the moorhens, and the crunch of fresh stems, until their mother called a halt.

'I think that's probably enough for the time being. You don't want to overdo it.' Orris began to complain, but she pre-empted him. 'The food will still be here when we come back. For now we have something else to do.' She looked from one to the other. 'It's time for me to show you the rest of the territory. Over the next few days you will want to explore, but under no circumstances must you leave my territory. Understood?'

'Why not?' asked Fern.

'Because it isn't safe. Now follow me.'

Their mother set off along the bank, keeping to well-trodden runs close to the water. She moved so quickly that it was difficult to keep up. Here and there she stopped, rising up on her haunches, listening, smelling. Then off again, following the track, hugging the bank, paddling in the shallows, bouncing across mats of plants, listening intently to every sound. Sylvan and the others scurried after her, pausing when she did, running as quickly as they could.

They grew accustomed to the
movement, the pauses under
cover, the dashes across open stretches.
The sights and sounds of the river flew by
until Sylvan felt almost as if he too were flowing
like Sinethis, rippling in the morning breeze.

A bird cried overhead. Its shadow fled before it
across the water. Their mother froze.

'Stop! Keep still, all of you.'

They halted right at the edge of the reeds. Overhead,
half hidden, a huge grey shape wheeled. Sylvan craned for a
clearer view, rising up on his hind legs. The bird cried once
more. And then his mother was on top of him, knocking him
to the ground. He was too startled even to squeak.

'I said to keep still,' she hissed. 'Now get under cover.
Move!'

She shoved them back, and they fled deeper into the reeds. The bird screeched again, closer this time. Through a gap in the dense grasses Sylvan could see a tiny patch of sky. For a split second it was eclipsed by an enormous shadow, then air beat down from above them, flattening the grass. The sunlight returned, filtered green down to the cowering water voles. A moment later there was nothing, only the sound of running waters. Somewhere a moorhen called. A breeze ruffled through, carrying with it a muted hum of insects. Sylvan hardly dared breathe. He moved his head a fraction for a glimpse of the others, huddled together, motionless beneath the vegetation. Even at this close distance they were difficult to see, their brown fur lost in the mud and dappled sunlight. He could just make out Orris's terrified expression and the shallow, quick rising of Aven's flanks. All of them gazed up through the shallow screen of reeds. The silence went on. Sylvan inched his head around, searching for any sign of the predator above them. Nothing but grey-blue sky, and swaying grass.

An orange flash stabbed down through the reeds. A beak: long, pointed, and vicious. It probed gently from side to side and withdrew. An instant later it stabbed again, closer to where Fern lay. It moved to the side, brushing Fern's fur. She uttered a tiny squeak. Her leg twitched.

'Keep still. Keep quiet.'

Their mother whispered so softly that Sylvan was unsure that he had heard. But her urgency was unmistakable. The beak withdrew. Long moments passed.

Then grasses were thrust aside with deft strokes, revealing a yellow eye with a black pupil set in a slender grey head. The eye roved, seeking its prey. Sylvan closed his eyes. *Please let it go away. Please don't let it see me. Please don't let it see the others. Please.*

THE RIVER SINGERS

The moments stretched and the tiny space filled with terror. Sylvan could almost taste it. He became a beating heart, quivering muscles. Every sense screamed at him to break cover, to run, to flee. But he clenched tighter, seeking anything which he could hold on to, anything to keep him from panic. And in that moment his mind filled with the sounds of the Great River, the burbling of her riffles, the swell lapping at the bare earth of the runs. *Sinethis*, he thought. *She shelters us. Mother said she shelters us.*

The bird let out an ear-splitting squawk. And then the air thrust downwards as powerful wings propelled it up and away. Sylvan opened his eyes to see its shadow slide from view. It cried again, more distantly this time. Sylvan got cautiously to his feet.

'W-what was that?'

'Heron,' said their mother, grimly. She faced her eldest son. 'This is not a game,

THE GREAT RIVER

Sylvan, and you are not a pup any more. It saw you. That's why it came for us. There are so many dangers out here and herons are one of the worst. Use your nose, use your ears, your wits. Don't take risks. Stay alive. Do you understand?'

Sylvan nodded, dumbly. She turned back to the others. 'And if they do see you, remember what I told you. *She shelters us in her waters and burrows.*' She gestured with her chin at the water. 'In the Great River they cannot catch you. Take your chance. Run, dive, swim, weave a path among the plants. Then find a burrow entrance. There is always one beneath the surface. Join with Sinethis and you will be safe. If not . . . '

She let the sentence hang. None of them spoke. She looked at the shocked faces of her offspring and her expression softened.

'Is everybody all right? Good. Come on, then. We're nearly there.'

She turned and ran off again along the water's edge. Sylvan followed, bewildered and scared. How could their mother have shaken off their near-death so quickly? He ran after her, alert to every sound and movement, a sense of threat urging him on, keeping him close. This time, though, they did not have far to go. She came to a halt, a little way from an old willow tree. The ground was bare beneath it, its roots spreading across the soil and down to the water. The thick branches cast a gloom over the water and stagnant specks swirled in the shade.

'Well,' said their mother, 'we're here. This is as far as my territory extends upflow. Remember this place, and be extra careful if you come here, especially if I'm not with you. Come on, have a look around.'

Their mother stepped out of the undergrowth. None of the rest of them moved. The dry soil looked terribly exposed. She put her head on one side and gave them a small smile.

'It's all right, dears,' she said, gently. 'Nothing bad happened. That heron got a bit closer than I'd normally like, but in the absence of anyone taking unnecessary risks'—here her gaze settled on Sylvan—'it's rare. You can't let these things trouble you. Come on out. It's fine.'

She walked to the tree and began checking the scents at the edge of her territory. Sylvan caught Aven's eye and saw in it a reflection of his own feelings. The experience had shaken him. Part of him longed to be safe in the nest and to forget about how, well, *big* everything was. But he knew that there was no going back. Somewhere, not quite smothered by the fear, he knew that he wouldn't even if he could. He was alive and he was outside. And it was amazing. He cast an eye up at the sky, as if expecting a heron at any moment. Then he swallowed and followed their mother into the open.

The boundary mark, the last outpost of their mother's territory, was plainly visible a little way beyond the grasses, on a raised and flattened tree root jutting out into the water. She sniffed at it for some moments then deposited some more droppings and scent and flattened the old markers with her hind feet. She nodded in some satisfaction.

'That should do it.' Then she moved a little further into the open and stopped by an older marker. She lowered her nose to it and frowned. She listened for a moment, then moved closer to the tree. She sniffed the air again.

'This is strange,' she muttered. 'There's something else here I don't recognize. Odd. Stoaty but not a stoat. Smells big. Near this tree.

And this marker's still untended. There's been no sign of her for days now.'

'Of who?' asked Sylvan.

'What, dear?' She seemed distracted. 'Oh. Mistress Esther.'

'Who's Mistress Esther?' said Fern.

'The female from the next territory. A good sort as far as it goes. Anyway, come and have a smell of this marker.'

She stepped back, letting Sylvan and the others gather round. Here at the edge of their mother's territory her familiar smell mingled with the unfamiliar odours of other River Singers. The old scent of the other female, Mistress Esther, overlaid the damp earth smell beneath the tree. Intermittent wafts of something musky and bitter assailed Sylvan's nose; the *not-stoat* smell, coming from the branches of the willow. Orris stepped away, cleaning his muzzle with both paws. Sylvan went over and nudged him.

'Stinks, doesn't it?'

'It's horrible,' said Orris. He gazed around meaningfully. 'All of it is.'

Sometimes Sylvan couldn't understand his brother. 'If you say so.'

'I do. Don't you?'

'No. It's a bit scary but . . . I don't know. It's great.'

Orris's look clearly said that he thought that Sylvan was a very special kind of halfwit. Sylvan gave up and joined Aven and Fern who were still investigating the boundary marker, chattering in low voices.

'What're you talking about?'

'Nothing,' said Fern, turning away. 'Female stuff. You wouldn't understand.'

Sylvan bristled, but Aven stepped in before he could speak. 'All right, nosy. We were talking about the female's scent. That's all.'

'Oh. What's so interesting about that?'

Fern gave him a withering look and preened her whiskers. 'Everything,' she said. 'Soon we will have territories of our own and then we'll need to know these things.'

'Right,' said Aven. 'And you won't have to worry about them. Being a dumb male.'

Somehow from Aven it was all right. Sylvan grinned. 'Well, if being a dumb male means that I don't have to spend my life with my nose in someone else's droppings, then that's fine with me.'

'You can learn a lot from the scents,' said Fern, defensively.

'Like what Mistress Esther had for dinner? No, thanks.'

Fern made an exasperated noise. 'No, like the fact that Mistress Esther's been gone a really long time.'

The river seemed to go quiet for a moment.

'Gone?' said Sylvan. 'Where did she go?'

Fern did not reply but looked over Sylvan's shoulder. Sylvan had not heard his mother come up, but now her reassuring presence was there behind them.

'Where did who go, dear?'

'Mistress Esther,' said Fern.

Their mother hesitated before answering. 'Well, I don't really know. She might be exploring further upriver. Or she might have moved territory. That happens sometimes. But I'm sure she'll be back soon.' She looked up at the light percolating through the leaves overhead. 'Right. I think that we've probably seen enough for one trip. It's getting brighter and the shadows are shortening. We'll head back to the burrow for now and come back out in the evening. It's easier to hide in long shadows, and there aren't so many predators.'

They followed her back along the bank, none of them speaking. It seemed to take a lot less time to get back to the main burrow, as if familiarity made the distance shorter, somehow. Their mother stood watch as they trooped in and headed down the tunnel to their sleeping chamber. Their nest of soft, dry grass was inviting. They curled up together, tired and thoughtful.

'Well, that was interesting,' commented Fern.

'Only interesting?' asked Sylvan, incredulous.

'Yes. I thought it was interesting.' She closed her eyes and began breathing deeply.

'So what did you think, then?' asked Aven.

'About which bit?' asked Orris. 'It was all horrible.'

'How can you say that?' said Sylvan.

'Easy. We were hardly out any time and we nearly got eaten by a heron. That put me off the rest of it.'

'Yeah, but we didn't get eaten, did we? And that won't happen every time.' Sylvan cast a sidelong glance at Orris's bulging belly. 'And the food's good.'

'There's food in the burrow.'

'Roots,' said Sylvan, dismissively. 'You can't live off roots.'

'I can try.' He sounded as if he meant it.

'It wasn't that bad,' said Sylvan.

'I'm not going out again.'

'Really?'

'Really.'

Sylvan snuggled in with the others. 'Well I am.'

The others were quickly asleep. But Sylvan's mind filled with memories and thoughts, and sleep would not come. He stared at the wall of the chamber, its lines worn smooth by generations of Singers. Here and there tiny roots had twisted out of the soil and been gnawed flat to the wall. Everything was cosy, warm, and familiar. In the midday lull the sounds of the Great River rang in his ears. Sinethis had been there his whole life, a hardly-considered background noise, a constant like their burrow, their mother, his brother and sisters. But now he had experienced her for himself, and she was changed for him for ever. She was more frightening than he had ever thought, but so much more wonderful. He closed his eyes and, for the first time, really *listened* to her, allowing the song to swell within him: bubbling top notes and deep rhythms, constant yet ever changing. She flowed into him, all vivid colours and sharp sensations. *We are River Singers*, he thought. *We are hers.* Somehow that felt good. It felt right. But even as he thought it he heard a strange note in her music, as if a single strand of the tune were out of place. He strained his senses trying to catch it. There: an odd, dissonant strand. It was almost engulfed in her vastness but it persisted. A cold, hard feeling. Something, somewhere, was wrong. *What is it?* he asked. And for an instant it seemed that words threaded their way through the Great River's music.

It is danger.

Sylvan's eyes snapped open. He shook his head to clear it. He listened again. The Great River sounded as she always had. The burrow looked normal, all solid earth walls and soft breathing. Strange. The words had sounded real. An odd feeling settled in him. Abruptly he wanted to leave the nest chamber. He needed space to think. For the second time that day, he eased himself out from among his siblings and crept off down the tunnel. Remembering his mother's warning not to leave the burrow, he instead followed the path up to the feeding hole. Their mother had taken them there once or twice to get a safe view of the world above when they were smaller. She had used the hole when she was pregnant because it was just large enough to get her head out of and graze on the grasses above. It would be the perfect place for him to find some air without getting into too much trouble.

Sylvan's feet carried him upwards until the tunnel began to lighten. As he approached, unfamiliar sounds echoed down to him. He slowed, listening intently. The sounds resolved into a voice, deep and rough. He could only make out some words, but it was the language of the Folk. Somewhere above a male Singer was talking. Sylvan had never met one. Intrigued, he crept forwards and the words became louder and more distinct, but still incomprehensible. Sylvan hesitated. He probably wasn't supposed to be doing this. But he was still inside the burrow, wasn't he? He inched closer and recognized with a small thrill another, more familiar, voice answering the male. His mother's. Sylvan hadn't thought that she knew any males. But then, he supposed, he didn't really know what she did when she left the burrow. He went as close as he dared, nosing his way up towards the feeding hole until he could just see them through the open circle of daylight. They were sitting together beneath a patch of bramble, a little distance away.

'. . . it's unnatural, I tell you,' the male was saying.

'Hush, Elon. Don't speak so loudly. You'll wake the children.'

'Apologies, Daphne. But it isn't normal. I'm worried; for me, and for you and the offspring. To be honest I'm worried for all of the Singers.'

'But surely it can't be that bad? We've been through hard times before. The Folk have always survived.' But Sylvan heard the uncertainty in her voice. It sent a chill through him.

'We have, I know. We all know that any day Sinethis

might choose us to be taken. This is our way and our enemies are many. But I have never heard of an enemy like this.'

His mother laughed but to Sylvan it sounded strained. 'Come on, Elon. That talk is just talk. It's probably just a big stoat or one of those horrible cat things. It could even be an otter. The old stories tell of them, don't they?'

'Perhaps. I have never seen one, but the stories have never described what I've seen. I roam widely these days, Daphne. Since the waters warmed, these banks have seemed to me unnaturally empty. The Folk are becoming sparse here. And Mistress Esther . . . '

Sylvan heard his mother's sharp intake of breath.

'Mistress Esther? What about her? I mean, I know she was taken but . . . '

A coldness settled in Sylvan's stomach. Mistress Esther wasn't away exploring. She was dead. Their mother had lied to them. But why? He pulled his attention back to the conversation.

The male said, ' . . . not by anything I have seen before. I was in her territory when it happened. I saw what it left.'

'What happened?' she asked, softly.

'I don't know. I have seen lots of things in my travels but . . . ' A wind blew through the grasses, muffling his words ' . . . was terrible. I think she had a litter. Who knows what became of them? It was bad, Daphne.'

Neither of the adults spoke for some moments. Then their mother said, 'What can I do?' Her voice was small and quiet.

'I don't know. I'm sorry. Be careful, I suppose. Try to stay safe. Trust in the Great River. What else can we do?'

The male stood with a slight scuffling sound. Abruptly Sylvan remembered where he was: exactly where he should not be and listening to a private conversation. He turned and scampered down to the nest chamber. He slunk in, unseen, and carefully cuddled up against the others. As he listened to their breathing his heart quietened, but a chilly unease lingered. He could make no sense of it. A new danger. Mistress Esther killed. Their mother scared. Before this morning, he had thought that the world would be fun, an adventure. And it was. It was wonderful. But part of that world had already gone wrong. There were real and unknown dangers out there. He needed to be careful. When finally he slept, it was as a far more thoughtful vole than he had been at dawn.

They went out that evening. Even Orris. Nettle roots, it seemed, were no match for the temptation of fresh stems. Sylvan said nothing to any of them about the feeding hole. He did not want them to be upset. He led the way down to the burrow entrance to

where their mother was waiting to usher them out into the cool evening air. The sun was low and the shadows deep. The Great River reflected yellow and orange dazzles as she flowed and the grasses bent in a small breeze. The Singers emerged sniffing at air which was laden with pollen and freshness. It was enough to make any vole forget his troubles.

'I thought we could have a little treat,' said their mother when they were all lined up beneath the thatch of reeds.

'What kind of treat?' asked Orris, suspiciously.

'The fun kind,' she said, smiling. 'You know, this side of the river is very nice but the food is much better on the other. So I thought we could explore over there a bit. There's more loosestrife and watercress and a lot more iris. It's part of the reason I fought so hard for this territory.'

Her last words were lost on Sylvan who was already dashing to the water's edge. They were going to swim across! He almost made it to the water before he remembered about the heron, and about being careful. He stopped dead, two feet poking out into the sunlight from under the plants. From behind him came the sound of a throat being cleared, meaningfully. He withdrew his feet, turned and sloped shamefacedly back to where the others were standing.

'I'm sorry.'

'Sylvan—'

'I know. I'm sorry. It won't happen again.'

'I wish I could believe that. Anyway, perhaps if certain voles can keep their enthusiasm under control we might all be able to cross the river. Safely. Do you think?'

'Yes, Mother.'

Their mother set off, followed by the others. Aven drew alongside Sylvan. 'Twit,' she said.

Sylvan ignored her and fell into line. They ran a little downflow, to a place where the sweet-grass formed a floating mat, extending out into the river. It was just firm enough to support a water vole. They picked their way across, following their mother's lead. The mat bounced beneath Sylvan's feet, sloshing cool water over his toes and wetting his tail. They left the overhead cover of reeds and herbs behind them, and emerged, squinting, into the evening sun.

'Any trouble,' said their mother, 'dive through the plants into the water. It'll be safe down there, but swim quickly and watch for pike.'

'Pike?' said Orris.

'Fish,' said Aven. 'Lots of teeth.'

Orris looked terrified.

'There is always danger,' said their mother, giving Aven a look. 'But a diving Singer is difficult to take. So this is a good place to eat.' She set off. 'As long as you're sensible, of course.'

Sylvan felt that the last addition may have been for his benefit. He concentrated on watching what he was doing, listening for trouble. When their mother reached the edge of the water proper, she paused and nibbled at a sweet-grass blade. She dropped it and mumbled something under her breath, so quietly that Sylvan doubted he had heard. And then she slid into the water. She floated buoyantly, paddling with her feet, tail streaming behind her, head and nose in clear air. Sylvan rushed to the water's edge to get a good view of her, barging Orris out of the way. To Sylvan the far bank seemed an incredible distance, but she made rapid progress to the trampled earth shore on the far bank. In no time she was out and grooming the water from her fur. She gave one final check for predators and called to her offspring.

'Sylvan?'

'Yes, Mother?'

'*Now* you can swim.'

Sylvan leapt into the Great River. Sinethis met him with a shock of cold; she flowed around and beneath him, buoying him, dragging at him, buffeting him, pulling him onward, pushing him downstream. He swam instinctively, eyes fixed on his goal: the small, dark hollow on the far shore. She was strong, so he angled himself to compensate, cutting across her. He paddled, shoving at her with his paws, half flowing, half fighting until the shade came to meet him, until he was within sight of his mother, reach of the bank, until he was pulling himself out of the water, panting and exhilarated.

'That was great,' he said. 'It was brilliant. I want to do it again.'

'Yes, dear. But please get out of the way so I can see how the others are doing.'

Sylvan stood aside to view their progress. Aven, looking even smaller than usual against the water, was already half-way across, swimming towards them. She arrived with eyes gleaming. Fern was next, stepping fastidiously over a knot of roots before easing into the water and swimming over with a determined expression. Orris hesitated, looking down fearfully at the river. He dipped a foot into the water and withdrew it, hastily.

'Come on, Orris,' shouted Sylvan.

'I don't want to. There might be pike.'

'Shouldn't worry,' muttered Aven. 'He's probably too fat to swallow.'

'Hush,' said their mother, sternly. Then she raised her voice. 'Orris, it will be fine, I promise. Just swim over.'

Behind Orris a large brown bird strutted along the riverbank. He spun round to face it. 'What's that?'

'It's a moorhen,' said their mother. 'It probably won't hurt you. Just don't get too close to it.'

Orris took a step back. The moorhen spied him and stopped. It raised a foot as if deciding what to do. Then it gave a loud cluck, put its head down and ran directly at him. Orris uttered a frightened squeak and dived headlong into the water.

Their mother laughed. 'Well, you were a bit close to its nest.'

Orris paddled furiously across, eyes fixed desperately on his goal. When he finally pulled himself out of the water, he was so miserable and bedraggled that even Aven could not bring herself to be sarcastic about it.

'Not having fun?' asked Sylvan sympathetically when Orris had shaken himself dry.

'Not really.'

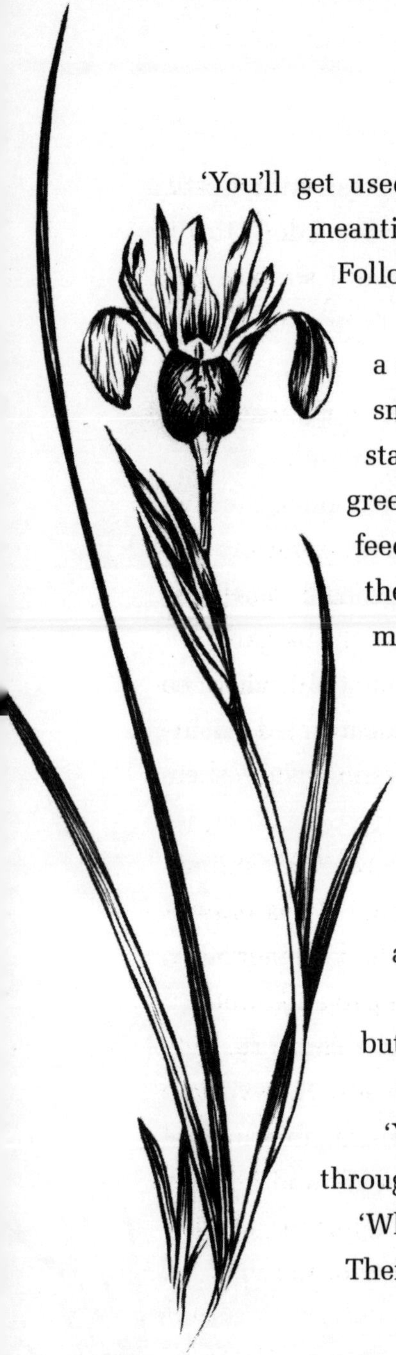

'You'll get used to it, dear,' said their mother. 'In the meantime I think that I can make it up to you. Follow me.'

It was a short run along the bank, past a couple of territory markers and around a small bend. They stopped in front of huge stands of iris leaves and bur-reed, all fresh, green, and succulent. Piles of chopped up feeding signs were everywhere, and behind them a vast array of juicy food. Sylvan's mouth began to water.

'This,' said their mother, 'is my favourite place to feed. Nothing much disturbs us here. The occasional male, but they know I have young. Otherwise it's nicely secluded, and close to deep water. And right now, my dears, it's all yours. Tuck in.'

Sylvan grabbed for the nearest stem, but then remembered something.

'Mother?'

'Yes dear?' the words were indistinct through a mouthful of greenery.

'What did you say just before you swam?'

Their mother swallowed. She looked almost

36

abashed, pushing at the remnants of some grass with a paw. 'Oh, that. Silly, really. It's an offering to Sinethis. I don't think that all of the Folk do it, but I always have. I suppose it's become a habit.'

'What are the words?' asked Fern.

'I said, "I offer myself as sacrifice. May your waters be kind." '

'What kind of sacrifice?'

'I never gave it much thought. But I suppose it means that we live our lives as a sacrifice to the Great River. And sometimes I think she needs reminding to keep her end of the bargain.'

'Oh,' said Sylvan. He didn't really understand what she meant. He put the thoughts aside, and concentrated on his hunger. He found some iris and began feeding. The others followed suit.

They feasted for some time and afterwards their mother led them away, heading further downstream. It was important, she said, that they should see both ends of the territory. They had not gone far, though, when she stopped and hunched low, listening intently. From up ahead came a sharp rustling noise, screened from view by a patch of reeds. A few more muted sounds followed. Then came the unmistakable noise of gnawing, and a reed being hauled downwards and chewed into sections. Their mother rose up on her haunches, staying as low as she could, scenting the breeze. Her nose twitched.

A small tilt of the head. Then she made an exasperated noise.

'Oh,' she said. 'It's her. How many times . . . Children, get behind me and under some cover, will you?'

The youngsters scampered to obey. When they were safely out of reach she raised her voice and squeaked a resigned-sounding challenge. The feeding sounds stopped. Sylvan and Aven craned for a closer look. A faint bustle in the reeds ahead resolved itself into the outline of a large female vole. She stopped a good distance away.

'Well,' called the stranger, sourly, 'I do believe that it is my dear neighbour. What a pleasant surprise on an evening. How are you, Daphne?'

The words were nice, thought Sylvan, but the way she said them was wrong. She didn't sound as if she meant them. 'Who's that, Mother?' he whispered.

'Mistress Valera.' His mother's tone too was odd: strained. She raised her voice. 'A fine evening to you, Valera. I was hoping we might meet each other today. Although I have to say that usually our encounters are a little further from my territory.'

'Ah, yes. We do seem to meet here quite a lot, don't we? It's a lovely thing to have such good neighbours. It was such a nice day that I thought I would pop along to the feeding place.'

Again the words were right, but only a hair short of openly hostile.

'*My* feeding place,' said their mother.

'Of course, dear. *Your* feeding place.' The two females faced each other with distaste. 'And what's this I see? You have young? Why, Daphne, what wonderful news. No wonder you have been absent for so long,' Valera continued, unpleasantly. 'But why ever did you not tell me? You should introduce us. Do please let them come closer so I can get a good look at them.'

With great reluctance, their mother stepped to the side to give Valera a view of her offspring. 'Don't move,' she whispered. Then louder, 'Young ones, this is Mistress Valera, our neighbour.'

'Oh, how dear they are!' Valera bared her teeth at Sylvan and his siblings. It wasn't quite a smile. 'What's your name, little one?' she asked, addressing Sylvan directly.

Sylvan looked questioningly at his mother, who gave a curt nod.

'Sylvan.'

'A male?'

Sylvan nodded.

'You wouldn't want to stray too far from home, I imagine? Not downstream onto anyone else's property?'

The question confused him. 'I would like to, Mistress Valera. It's good to explore.'

'Oh, deary me. Not an advisable attitude. Not advisable at all. But males will be males, I suppose. And who are these others?'

'My brother and sisters.'

'I never would have guessed,' she said, drily. 'Do they have names?'

'Yes,' said Sylvan, taking the question literally.

Valera gave him a hard look and turned back to their mother. 'Well, Daphne you *have* done well getting such a healthy litter so far in life. Especially considering what happened to the last lot.'

Their mother's back stiffened.

'Anyway, listen to me going on. I'm sure you have your paws full keeping these fine young voles from harm, teaching them about the world and things. And here I am wasting your precious time. Don't let me detain you.'

Their mother smiled tightly. 'Oh, you're not detaining me, Valera. I was just showing my family the boundaries of their home. Or I would be if we had got there yet. The edge of my territory, as we all know, is still a little way downstream, and I wouldn't dream of leaving before they're thoroughly familiar with it. It would be terribly impolite of me not to educate them about their limits. Perhaps we could all walk down to the marker and show them together? And, of course, when you finally have a litter of your own, you must feel free to return the favour.'

Valera did not respond. Their mother continued, 'It would be so nice to see you with children some day, Valera. To be honest I rather thought that you'd have some by now, but there's no point in rushing these things. All in good time.'

Sylvan couldn't see what his mother had said that was wrong, but Mistress Valera's whiskers tensed. Her head came up and she bared her teeth again.

'Yes, Daphne. All in good time. Well, good day to you. It has been lovely to, ah, visit your property. A pleasure as ever.' She whipped round and with a rustle was gone.

Their mother said nothing but it seemed to Sylvan that she had a slightly triumphant look on her face.

'Nasty old trout,' commented Aven to Fern.

'Hush, girls,' said their mother. 'Don't speak ill of other voles. Especially not Mistress Valera.'

'Why not?' asked Fern.

Their mother cast a look in the direction from which Mistress Valera had disappeared. 'Just don't, please. She's enough trouble as it is. Right. I think we're almost done. We'll take a short trip down to my boundary mark and refresh the scent. That way even Mistress Valera, who apparently has no sense of smell, will know where it is. Then I think we can probably return to the burrow and get some sleep.'

She paused.

'And yes, Sylvan, that does mean we get to swim again.'

The terror came in the night. It came with swiftness. It came with teeth.

Sylvan awoke with Orris at his shoulder. The burrow was dark and Sylvan was dazed from sleep. He began complaining, muzzily, but Orris silenced him.

'Quiet. Listen,' he hissed.

Sylvan listened. He could hear nothing but their sisters' breathing and

the ever present sound of the Great River. He peered into the darkness but could see nothing. Moments stretched away and Sylvan relaxed. There was nothing out there. Orris had probably had a nightmare or been scared by an owl or something. He was about to say as much when he too caught a faint noise. He strained his senses and it came again. Unmistakably, somewhere in the burrow, something was sniffing. He heard a soft scatter of footfalls. Then more sniffing. Sylvan's hackles rose.

'What is it? Weasel?' asked Orris.

Sylvan shivered. A weasel in the burrow was a Singer's nightmare. They could be escaped, he knew, but the only way was the Great River. On land they would take you. He shook his head.

'Don't know. But I don't like it.'

Silence eddied around their tiny space. They heard nothing for long moments. But then the sniffing sound came again and feet padded directly below them, in a tunnel beneath their chamber. More sniffing, horribly audible through the floor of the nest.

'It's in the burrow. It's going to find us.' Orris's voice was filled with panic.

'Quiet,' Sylvan hissed. 'It'll hear us. You have to stay quiet.'

Orris let out a low moan. 'Oh, please don't let it find us.'

Sylvan put a restraining paw on his brother. The sniffing

noise stopped. Sylvan could almost picture the creature with an ear cocked, listening. Nothing. Then another padding of feet. It was heading off down another branch, getting further from the nest. Sylvan sagged with relief and turned to Orris. But Orris had curled up on himself and was rocking with his paws over his eyes.

'It's going to find us, it's going to find us,' he repeated.

Sylvan turned an uneasy eye to the nest entrance and kept his paw on Orris's back.

'It won't find us. Just keep quiet.'

But even as he spoke, the footfalls came louder than before, from a different tunnel. Sylvan's heart began to thump. The creature had found the back way that led up to the nest. The sniffing and padding grew louder, more eager, coming closer. Another, brief, silence. Then more steps, just outside the chamber. Then silence. Sylvan could not move, frozen to the spot with fear. Orris was silent but he could feel him shaking. A patch of darkness lightened, resolved itself into the tip of a nose. Sniffing, sniffing, unbelievably loud in the enclosed space. Sylvan could feel the rancid air of the creature's breath as it filled the entrance.

Their nest had become a trap. Two more sniffs. A pause, with an air of unspeakable triumph. Then the nose surged forwards, followed by a black head and two shining eyes, and teeth bared in a wicked smile. Orris gasped and shrank against the back wall of the chamber. Sylvan too fled to the wall. Fern awoke with a scream. She and Aven dashed to where Sylvan cowered and huddled between him and Orris.

The creature snaked its head from side to side, taking its time, sizing its prey. It had no need to hurry. Sylvan watched the eyes as they flicked from vole to vole, unmistakably coming to rest on Orris's trembling form. The creature's grin broadened. Without thinking, Sylvan rose up on his hind legs, ready to fight with everything he had. The creature whirled and snapped at him with horrible speed. Sylvan hurled himself aside, collided with the wall, and lay winded on the earth. Every instinct screamed at him to get up, to face it. But he could hardly breathe. He could not move. He closed his eyes. He heard the soft impact of the creature's paws on the soil. The creature's breath ruffled his fur. He could almost feel the mouth gaping, the teeth gleaming . . .

'Children!'

Their mother's scream echoed in the tunnel.

The creature withdrew a fraction.

'Children! I'm coming.'

The sounds of her paws grew louder. She was heading straight for the nest chamber. Sylvan rolled to his feet. He wanted to shout, to warn her, anything. He took a shuddering breath but no words came out. The creature raised its head and scented the air a final time. Then its teeth snapped together once and it was gone, flowing away down the tunnel. Sylvan found his voice. He screamed things he couldn't understand, yelling his terror into the burrow air; anything to warn her, to give her a chance. Fern and Aven joined him, squeaking and screaming, cowering together against the burrow wall. Only Orris, rocking to himself, was quiet.

When at last they fell silent, the burrow was still. No sound but the muted flow of the Great River remained. And although they listened all the long night, they heard nothing more.

Sylvan led them warily out to feed in the morning. Their mother was not in the burrow. The creature's prints and odour were everywhere, overlaying the clean earth. It was the same scent they had smelt by the tree at the top of the territory: acrid, stoaty, bad. Sylvan had explored for longer and further than the others, running here and there, prying into the forgotten places of the burrow. He found nothing. Finally exhaustion forced him to give in and return to where the others were waiting. As he trudged the path to the main chamber, his gaze fell on a patch of fresh earth, fallen from the tunnel wall. In the earth was a pawprint, large with five toes. Five toes: weasel or stoat, their mother had told them. Beware. Danger. But this print was too big, and a strange shape. Not a stoat, then. Something else. Something worse. He sniffed it and recoiled from the stench. The tunnel wall here looked odd. Twin scratch marks, deeply incised on either side, ran down its length. They might have been made from something scrabbling at the wall, trying to gain purchase. It was from these that the soil had fallen. Sylvan held a paw up to the scratches and quickly withdrew it. Apart from his smaller size, the scratches could have come from his own paw. Tears stung his eyes. A horrible feeling welled in him. What could he do now? Their mother was gone and possibly . . . no, best not to think it.

Sylvan stood in the tunnel, head hanging, eyes closed. Everything felt twisted, as if the world was broken and couldn't be put right. He wanted it all to go away. He wanted to curl up and stay there. But he couldn't, he knew. He was the oldest of the family, now. He needed to be strong, not just for him but for all of them. He stared at the scratches on the wall for a long moment. He felt the sorrow rise up in him again, and he fought it down. He brushed the scratches from existence, carefully smoothing the tunnel back to how it should be. Then he walked to the main chamber.

The others looked up as he entered. Fern made a soft noise and looked down at her feet. Aven stared straight ahead, blinking. Orris barely moved, but hunched in a little more on himself.

'No sign,' said Sylvan. 'I've looked everywhere.'

'I'm sure that she'll come back,' said Fern. She sounded anything but sure.

'Maybe,' said Sylvan, carefully. 'But until she does we're on our own.'

'You think she might?' The hope in Fern's voice was almost unbearable. What could he say? He couldn't tell them about the scratches. Not yet. Tears welled up again but he blinked them back.

'It's possible,' he said. 'But we need to stay together. We need to feed like she taught us.'

'I don't want to eat,' said Orris.

'We have to. We have to be strong.'

'What if Mother comes back?' asked Aven.

'Then she'll find us outside, feeding. And she'll be proud of us.'

So the others followed him out. They huddled at the water's

edge. Fern and Aven said little, eating
mechanically. Orris did not speak at all,
not eating until Sylvan made him. Even then,
he stared at Sylvan blankly before turning to
the plants and beginning to gnaw. Occasionally
a sharp noise, a splash from a fish or the cluck of
a coot, made them dash for the burrow. From time
to time one of them would hear a softer sound, raise
a head and gaze hopefully into the reeds. But although
they waited all morning, their mother never came.
When they finished feeding they returned to the
burrow. The tunnel walls echoed emptily back at
them. They found a side chamber, not their nest,
and slept fitfully.

In the evening they returned to the water.
Again they fed in silence until disturbed by
a rustle in the reeds and a brown-furred shape
bustling through the grasses. They rose
to their haunches, and then dropped
down in bitter disappointment. It was
a water vole, but it was not their
mother. The newcomer stopped
a little distance away and
surveyed the group with
a smug smile.

'Well, well. Deary, deary me,' said Mistress Valera. 'I thought I hadn't seen Daphne today. Valera, I said to myself, you haven't seen your delightful neighbour in almost an entire day. And that isn't like my dear Daphne at all, now is it? So, being a good neighbour, I thought that I would pop along and make sure that nothing terrible had befallen her.'

Sylvan glared at the newcomer, outraged. She shouldn't be in their mother's territory. Mistress Valera returned his gaze evenly.

'Mother's just gone for a while. She'll be back. Soon.' Sylvan's voice shook a little.

'Really, my dear?' Mistress Valera sidled closer. 'And where has she gone, exactly?'

'I don't know. But she'll be back.'

'Well maybe you're right, dear. I do hope that nothing nasty has happened to her. By the way, are all of you youngsters all right? It was quite a commotion last night, wasn't it?' Mistress Valera's tone was pure sweetness. Sylvan kept silent. 'I mean what with all of that rushing about and screaming. I heard it all the way down in my territory. It was quite terrible,' she continued. Sylvan's claws dug into the earth. 'Anyway, just in case she doesn't return, I wondered whether I should perhaps extend my protection over her territory for a little while? You wouldn't want any less scrupulous females sniffing about her property, now would you.'

Fern said, 'Thank you, Mistress Valera. That's very kind.'

Sylvan rounded on Fern. 'No it isn't. She shouldn't be here.'

'You should mind your manners,' snapped Mistress Valera.

'And you should go away and leave us alone,' said Sylvan.

Mistress Valera considered the small male in front of her, head on one side. She appeared to come to a conclusion. She showed her teeth.

'Yes. Perhaps I should go back. I'm sure that four wise young voles like you will have no difficulty surviving another night. I'll come back tomorrow to check on you. And if, in the meantime, your mother does happen to reappear, you can tell her how well I looked after things for her.' She leaned closer until she was almost head to head with Sylvan. She dropped her voice to a whisper. 'But I don't think she'll be back. *I* will be, though. Never fear about that.'

Mistress Valera raised her head and surveyed the river bank with a proprietorial air. Then she turned and waddled slowly back towards her own burrow. Sylvan glowered after her retreating form.

'You should have been nicer to her,' said Fern.

'Why?'

'Because if Mother doesn't come back, this will be her territory.'

'No it won't,' said Sylvan. 'We're still here. It's ours.'

'That doesn't matter,' said Fern. 'We're too small to fight her. But maybe we could persuade her to give us a bit of space. If we were nice to her.'

Sylvan stared at his sister. He wanted to shout at her, to tell her that they were strong, and that she shouldn't talk that way. But she had a point: they weren't big enough to fight. And without their mother . . . He shook his head.

'She'd never let us stay,' he said, quietly.

'Sylvan's right,' said Aven. 'She's not exactly going out of her way to make us feel wanted. If she takes over the territory the first thing she'll do is to drive us out. That's the way females are.'

Sylvan had never before thought of what would happen if their mother was gone. None of them had. He only knew the way things should be; and that did not include Mistress Valera. The new possibility of losing their home opened before him, black and frightening.

'Say she makes us leave,' he said. 'What then?'

'Well, what do you think?' said Aven. 'We'll have no burrow, nowhere to sleep, and nothing to eat. No other female will let us into their territory. It's not going to be fun, is it?'

'We'd have to find somewhere that nobody owns,' said Fern.

Orris had been following the conversation with wide eyes. 'But Mother's just gone away for the day, right? That's what you said. She's coming back. Isn't she, Sylvan?'

Sylvan thought about the scratch marks on the burrow wall. He avoided Orris's gaze.

'I don't know, Orris. But if Mother doesn't come back, we can't let Mistress Valera have the territory. We'll have to fight her for it.'

He looked at the frightened faces of his siblings. He wished he felt half as brave as he sounded.

'It's the only way. Agreed?'

They nodded, even Orris.

'Good. Then we should keep eating. We are going to need to be strong.'

That night they slept in the same side chamber as before, because it had two entrances and an easy escape to the water. They took it in turns to stand guard, Sylvan taking the first watch. As the others fell into an exhausted slumber, he sat in deep thought, listening in the falling darkness. The events of the last two days played ceaselessly in his mind. How had so much changed in such a short time? Yesterday life had been a game. Now he was a small, scared vole, huddling in a burrow, responsible for his siblings. And tomorrow they

would have to fight or be driven from their home and into the unknown. Only the sound of Sinethis was the same; constant and carefree. For a moment, Sylvan felt an irrational hatred of the Great River. Ever since they had first gone out, things had been falling apart. This was her fault. *We are River Singers, Water Folk, children of the Great River*, his mother had said. *She shelters us in her waters and burrows.* But where had Sinethis been last night? What help had she provided for her children? But then Sylvan remembered his waking dream— had it only been yesterday?—when as the others slept he had heard Sinethis's song. He recalled the note of discord. He remembered the words that had sprung into his mind: *It is danger.* Had that, somehow, been a message? Had Sinethis been trying to warn him?

Sylvan blinked in the darkness. A speck of hope blossomed. They were the children of the Great River, he thought. If that were true, then perhaps she could help them. He closed his eyes once more. *Please*, he prayed. *Please let our mother come back. Please don't let Mistress Valera take our home.*

He listened hard, hoping for any response. But her song remained as it was, careless and distant. He remembered how she had sounded before, the single discordant thread twisting through her. He hunted for that sound. There. There amidst the churning and running of her melody was a tiny thread, almost drowned. But it was there: unwelcome and out of harmony with the rest. He concentrated on it. *Please help.* Words bubbled into his mind. This that you ask, they seemed to say, this is not my way.

So Sinethis did not care about their loss. Why would she? She is as old as stones and our song with her is brief as summer. *We live our lives as a sacrifice to the Great River,* their mother had said, *perhaps she needs reminding to keep her end of the bargain.* At the time Sylvan hadn't known what she had meant. But now, alone at the edge of his world, he crept towards an understanding. *Is this,* he demanded, *how you keep your bargain? Fine then. If what I asked is not your way, then give me the strength to fight. Give me the courage to look after the others. At least give me that. If not, I'll do it without you. But I **will** do it.*

Something in her song shifted. She grew louder in his mind, and it seemed to him that a skein of music wove itself around and through him. It bound itself into him, raising his head, straightening his back, stiffening his resolve. This is my way, it said. Flow with me. Be as I am. Be yielding but strong, swift and implacable. Flow with me. You will need to swim, to fight. But flow with me. This is my way.

Then the feeling was gone and the Great River was once more muted through the burrow walls. Sylvan shook his head, unsure if he had heard correctly. But something new had lodged in him; a determination that whatever happened to them tomorrow, or the day after, they would be together. They would survive.

'Still here, are you? And no Daphne. Dear me. How unfortunate.'

Sylvan and the others had spent an excruciating day with nothing to do but force themselves to eat, watch, and wait, hoping for any sign of their mother, dreading the return of their neighbour. It was Mistress Valera who turned up, just as the sun was going down. They were outside, making the most of the shadows, when her sharp features thrust through the vegetation. She waddled right up to the burrow entrance, pausing only to sniff at the burrow marker.

'This scent is very old,' she said. 'What a pity.' Then she started walking towards the burrow. Sylvan quickly ran in front of her, blocking her way.

'Where are you going?' said Sylvan.

Mistress Valera feigned surprise. 'Why, into my burrow, of course.'

Sylvan felt his heart begin to race. 'It's not your burrow.'

'Oh? And whose is it, then?'

Sylvan indicated his siblings, who had fallen in behind him. 'It's ours. And when Mother gets back it'll be hers again.'

Mistress Valera gave a snort of derisive laughter.

'Hah! "When Mother gets back",' she mimicked. 'You listen to me, little one: your mother's not coming back. No female leaves her territory untended for two whole days. Your mother is dead. This is my territory and you'd better get used to it.'

Sylvan heard Orris gasp at her words. He did not look round, but remained where he was between Mistress Valera and the entrance.

'Our mother may be dead,' he said, his voice hardly shaking, 'but that means that this is our territory, not yours.'

Mistress Valera's eyes narrowed. 'And how do you work that out, little one? Which of you will challenge me for it?'

'We shouldn't have to,' said Fern. 'You have enough space in your territory. You don't need this one. Why not just leave us alone?'

Mistress Valera smiled humourlessly. 'Oh, yes, that's a wonderful idea, deary. Of course that's exactly what I'll do. I'll leave you here: two females who will be adults before I know it. And you'll divide this territory between you and you'll have young of your own and suddenly all this space won't be enough. And then you'll start looking at old Mistress Valera's territory, thinking "Look at all the river she has, and we have so little and surely she won't miss it" and then I'll be finding markers springing up in my patch, and my territory getting smaller and my children having nowhere to go.'

She fixed them with a horrible stare. 'So, no. If it's all right with you, I prefer to nip the problem off at the bud.' She leant forwards. 'And you, little ones, are the bud I intend to nip. Now run away like good little voles.'

'No,' said Sylvan.

'I beg your pardon, deary?'

'I said no.'

'That's what I thought you said. They never learn. Oh dear.'

Mistress Valera rose up, almost as if she were stretching or scenting the breeze, but then lunged forward, teeth bared in a snarl, battering at Sylvan with her paws. Sylvan, taken by surprise, was knocked to the side. He landed in a heap and struggled to his feet. Aven, eyes wide, was next in line. Despite her tiny size she did her best to fight. But she was beaten away, sprawling and bleeding from a scratch in her flank. Mistress Valera paused, eyeing the remaining two. She began to stalk forwards. Orris and Fern backed away. Sylvan rushed to Aven's side.

'Are you OK?'

She picked herself up, wincing. 'Fine. Go and help the others.'

But Orris and Fern were already running towards them, fleeing a gleeful Mistress Valera. They stopped where Sylvan and Aven were standing and the four of them faced their assailant. Mistress Valera was out of breath, but her eyes glinted triumphantly.

'Run,' she screamed. 'Run away, little Singers.'

Sylvan hesitated, and in that moment's indecision, Mistress Valera was on him once more. She bowled him over and her teeth snapped at his exposed neck, making him jerk away. She snapped at

him again and her paws raked at his face. Abruptly Sylvan realized that she was no longer trying to drive them off. She was trying to kill him. He lashed out, squeaking a challenge. One of his hind feet connected with her nose, making her flinch. He rolled free and dashed along the bank, yelling at the others, desperately trying to put distance between him and Mistress Valera. The others followed, running in blind panic, fleeing upstream after him, along the bank, through the waters, past unused boundary markers and on, on through vegetation which whipped at their faces. At their heels panted Mistress Valera, still screaming, never more than a few paces behind.

They ran until their sides were aching and their muscles burned. They began to gain ground, but the crashing of Mistress Valera through the undergrowth behind them was still perilously close. To Sylvan it appeared as if the grasses were hurling themselves at him, making him duck and weave. He stumbled and rolled, not daring to stop. Every second he felt as if her teeth were closing on his haunch, her paws raking at him. They ran and the crashing sounds behind them receded. Behind him Sylvan could hear Orris

shouting something about Mistress Valera, but still Sylvan ran on with grim determination. Through the chaos of shapes in the falling twilight he recognized the tree at the upper end of their mother's territory and his nostrils filled with a stoaty stink. He stopped dead. Aven pulled alongside.

'What are you doing? Run! She's only stopped for a second. If she catches us we're dead. Run!' But Sylvan grabbed for her, forced her back. Orris and Fern stumbled up behind them, panting.

'What? What's wrong?'

Sylvan hissed at them for silence.

'Quiet,' he said. 'Look.'

They followed his gaze. From amongst the roots of the tree a lithe, black shape detached itself from the shadows. Eye-shine flashed green for a second and vanished. The shape padded forwards and cocked its head, listening, almost invisible in the dusk.

'Move,' whispered Sylvan. 'Get back.' As silently as they could they backed away into a patch of reeds. They could see the beast padding this way and that, head up, alert.

'It heard us,' whispered Sylvan.

The beast raised its head and scented the air. Its head moved this way and that, and then it put its nose to the ground and padded towards them.

'What do we do?' asked Orris. Sylvan shook his head. He could not think. He stared in horror as it closed on them, sniffing out their hiding place. He heard a rustle behind him and whirled to catch sight of Fern's tail disappearing into the vegetation, heading back the way they had come. He looked back at the beast which had risen up on its hind legs, listening intently. It had heard the rustle. Anger and sorrow welled up in him. Fern had run away. And she had endangered all their lives.

The creature stepped forward, confident that its prey was near. It was so close that Sylvan could see the white patch beneath its chin and the sharpness of its teeth as it grinned. It sniffed again, stepped again. Its nose parted the grasses immediately in front of Sylvan's face. Sylvan shrank back and closed his eyes. His chest heaved. This time, surely, it was the end.

Then, somewhere behind them, bedlam broke loose. Sylvan's eyes snapped open in time to see Fern exploding past

their hideaway, sprinting along the bank as fast as she could go. Crashing after her was Mistress Valera, shouldering her way through the undergrowth, squeaking obscenities at the fleeing youngster. The beast started in surprise and then was gone, dashing with terrible speed after the plump form of Mistress Valera. Voles and creature disappeared into the gloom.

A brief silence. Then a horrified squeak and a distinct plop, as of a water vole diving into the Great River, followed by a much louder splash. Then splashing and squeaking until there was a single, abrupt, piercing shriek.

Night noises closed in, disturbed only by a gentle sloshing which faded to nothing. Then there was quiet.

Sylvan, Aven, and Orris could not move. They were struck dumb with horror, not daring to imagine whether Fern was dead or alive, or whether the beast would now come for them. Beyond the Great River the sun set and the far bank became lost in the twilight. The air grew chill. An owl hooted overhead. They moved closer together. A faint rustle sounded, a little way off. It could have been the breeze, but it was not. It came again, a little closer: something small moving wearily along the bank, stumbling towards them, shoving through the grasses and falling, gasping, into the middle of their group.

Sylvan's heart swelled with joy. It was Fern. They crowded around their sister, nestling against her, whiskers twitching with delight. Eventually she recovered enough to say, 'It worked. It got Mistress Valera. She's gone.'

'You did that on purpose?' asked Sylvan, shocked.

Fern nodded.

'Nice one.'

Fern smiled, weakly. Then she said, 'Mistress Valera. She jumped into the Great River. It followed her. It caught her in the water. How could it do that?'

'It can't have,' said Aven. 'Are you sure?'

Sylvan heard the shock in Aven's voice and knew how she felt. Sinethis was their final protection. No enemy from the land could catch the Singers when they gave themselves to her. It was part of the promise. If this thing could hunt in the water . . . It didn't bear thinking about.

'Yes.' Fern closed her eyes and curled up. 'Tired,' she said. In seconds she was asleep.

Some of Sylvan's own tiredness had drained away, replaced by joy at seeing his sister alive. Overhead an owl hooted once more. He tensed, realizing that night had fallen and that they were still in the open. They needed shelter. They needed him to be strong.

'We need to find cover. There must be a burrow around here somewhere.'

'There's one further back. I saw it when we came up here with . . . Mother.' Aven's voice tailed off. Sylvan had no time to think about that.

'Good,' he said, briskly. 'Let's find it. Come on: you and Orris lend me a paw. Let's get Fern to safety.'

Between them they roused Fern and escorted her, barely able to walk, back along the bank. Nearly hidden beneath a fringe of water mint was an old burrow entrance with a few scattered droppings outside. The droppings smelt faintly of their mother. This must have been one of her old refuges. Between them they cajoled and shoved the sleepy Fern up the passage to a scruffy but secure nest. She curled up in some dried grasses and was instantly asleep. Aven and Orris slumped against the wall, almost as exhausted.

'Go ahead,' Sylvan told them. 'Sleep. I'll keep watch for a bit.'

'What if that . . . thing comes back, Sylvan?' said Orris. 'It could follow our scents here. It could find us.'

Sylvan felt a flash of anger. They were in a burrow, weren't they? They were alive and relatively safe. He was nearly exhausted himself. What else could Orris possibly expect him to do? He could not find the words to reply.

Aven said, 'We're probably OK, Orris. It ate Mistress Valera. I don't reckon it'll be hungry for a while.'

Sylvan stared at her. Then, for some reason, he began to

chuckle. It began deep within his belly then swelled into laughter until he could hardly breathe. It didn't feel like a real laugh, though. It had an edge of hysteria. It was as if all the things that had happened to them over the last days had decided to use that moment to pour uncontrollably out of him. He squeezed his eyes together, nearly crying with the hilarity.

'What's so funny?' asked Aven, her small frame radiating bewilderment.

Sylvan rolled onto his side, paws in the air, powerless to stop it. Aven's confusion and Orris's open mouth just made it all the funnier.

'I'm sorry,' he gasped, ' . . . it's just that . . . you said it won't be hungry . . . '

'Yes,' said Aven, patiently.

'Well . . . d-did you see the size of her bottom? That'd keep anyone going.'

Watching him rolling on the floor, a rueful grin spread across Aven's face. 'I don't know,' she said. 'I reckon Mistress Valera would've tasted really bitter. She might have ruined its appetite.'

'Yeah,' said Sylvan. 'If we're . . . we're lucky she might have put it off voles for good.' He collapsed again, and this time Aven joined him, tears in her eyes and her breath coming in thick sobs.

Orris did not join them. He looked from his brother to his sister, walked a little way off, and hunched in on himself. When they had recovered, and the laughter had subsided, he said, 'It took Mother, you know. I don't think it's very funny.'

Sylvan sobered up. He let out a shuddering breath.

'I know it took Mother, Orris. And I'm sorry. It's just . . . ' He had no words to describe it. He looked in desperation to Aven. She too was now looking serious.

'Look, we all feel the same,' she said. 'I don't know why that was funny, but it was. Maybe we just needed to laugh about something, that's all. I'm sorry too. But we weren't being horrible, we really weren't.'

'We're alive and we're together and it's been a hard day,' said Sylvan. 'Maybe we should get some sleep. Then in the morning we can start making our territory right again. OK?'

'OK,' said Orris.

'Good. You go ahead. I'll keep a lookout for a while.'

'Aren't you tired?' asked Aven.

'I'll be fine,' said Sylvan.

He watched them as they nestled alongside Fern, and as their breathing became regular. Now the laughter, and his joy at seeing Fern, had subsided, tiredness threatened to overwhelm him. Sylvan had said that he would watch over them, and that he would be strong. He meant to keep his word. But as the night claimed their little burrow, one thought ran again and again through his tired mind: it was still out there. It had taken Mother and Mistress Valera. If they stayed in the territory, how long would it be before it came for them?

Sylvan had slept little and woken early. He padded off alone, down to the water to feed. The morning was fine and cool, and every leaf shone green-gold in the sun. He sipped at dew which had collected between a sweet-grass leaf and its stem, and then munched on its soft parts, savouring the process.

'Greetings, young Singer. A fine morning, isn't it?'

Sylvan jumped. It was a male Singer.

'Yes it is. And who are you?' said Sylvan, suspiciously, putting down his grass stem.

The male regarded Sylvan evenly. 'I'm not someone who's accustomed to being spoken to like that. I hope we're not going to have words.'

'Words? What sort of words?'

'Savage ones.' The tone was mild but the male gave off a sense of hardness. Sylvan was abruptly aware of their size difference and the sting of the scratches on his flank from Mistress Valera.

'Anyway,' continued the male. 'It's your mother I wish to speak to. Where is she?'

'She's gone,' said Sylvan. He raised his chin and looked the other in the eye.

'Another?' said the male, almost to himself. Then he said, 'I'm sorry. She was a fine female.'

Sylvan could think of no reply. He did not want to hear a strange male talking about his mother. He frowned. 'What did you mean "another"?' he asked.

'It may be nothing.'

'But it might not be. If you know something, you should tell me.'

The male scrutinized him for some moments, as if weighing up how much Sylvan was worth.

'Very well,' he said. 'You will be adult soon enough and the Great River has entered your life. And you're certainly feisty. Let's find some cover and I'll tell you my thoughts.'

A little way from the bank edge was a dense clump of brambles. The male checked for danger and then ran into it. Sylvan followed him into the brambles. The shade was cool

and the spiked stems formed a low roof, just high enough for the two water voles.

The male looked around him approvingly. 'This is a good shelter. I have used it on many occasions. But to business. My name is Elon.'

He saw the expression on Sylvan's face. 'Ah. My name is familiar to you, perhaps?'

Sylvan nodded, slowly. 'Yes. I think I heard you talking . . . to our mother. You were saying something about Mistress Esther. That she was killed by something.'

'You have sharp ears,' said the male gravely. 'But that's no bad thing in a Singer. I'll tell you about Mistress Esther, but first I must tell you about the Great River. You must understand how things should be.'

Sylvan nodded. Elon said, 'Very well, then. Once, I was young like you. I left my mother and sisters as a Singer should.

I spent my days ranging, feeding, and courting. I met females, fathered young. I met males, and we fought. The days were long, the sun was warm, and these banks were filled with Singers. We all thought it would never end. Whether we angered the Great River I don't know, but she rose up and flooded our burrows. And then, when her waters dropped, the grasses died, the banks hardened, and the days grew cold and short. We burrowed more deeply and gnawed on roots in the darkness. Many Folk died. When at last the days lengthened, the air began to warm and we emerged to find the banks emptier than they had been. It was a terrible time.'

Sylvan listened, wide-eyed. Their mother had never spoken of this, but she must also have lived through it.

Elon continued, 'These things are told in Singers' tales. Sinethis's moods have come before and will come again. Always they pass, though. It is her way. And because it is her way it is also ours.'

Sylvan struggled to take it all in. 'But now you think that something is wrong? Something else?'

'I do. The waters have long since warmed and we have renewed our courting. I have fathered young. But still the banks are empty around me. Females disappear with their litters. Males vanish, never to be seen. I hear whispers of a new enemy; a black creature, more vicious than the others. Things are not as they should be. Perhaps the Great River is still angry. Or perhaps this is something beyond her. But it seems to me that the whispers are true: the Folk here are dying.'

A feeling of hopelessness twisted in Sylvan. Their mother was gone and their world was ending and he was too small to do anything. But he remembered his brother and sisters, and he remembered the feel of the Great River twining in him, the words she had sung to him. This was not beyond Sinethis. She would help him be strong. She had said so. He looked up.

'I saw the beast,' he said. 'It killed our mother and it killed Mistress Valera.'

Elon drew a sharp breath. 'You saw it?'

Sylvan nodded. He described the creature, how it had smelt and how it had come into their burrow and chased Mistress Valera in the river. When he had finished, the male looked serious.

'I have escaped many enemies but never one like this. If it swims as you say, and enters our burrows, then the Great River surely has abandoned us.' Elon stood up and gazed out through the screen of brambles. 'Thank you for your information. I must leave you now. I have my way to go, and you have yours. What will you do?'

Sylvan shook his head. 'I don't know,' he said. 'We wanted to stay here, now Mistress Valera's gone.'

'Then I wish you luck,' said the male. 'Perhaps Sinethis will relent. Perhaps the beast will leave. But until then these waters are no longer safe. Perhaps it is time to leave. I don't know. Your decision is private, between you and Sinethis. Give my respects to your siblings. Take care of them for me.'

And before Sylvan could say anything Elon dashed off. He disappeared with a rustle and was quickly hidden in the plants. Sylvan closed his eyes. After everything they had been through he desperately needed a chance to stop, to think, to grieve. But if Elon was to be believed, their troubles were only just beginning. *Perhaps it is time to leave*, he had said. Sylvan picked up his fallen sweet-grass stem and chewed it, thoughtfully. *Perhaps it is time to leave.*

'What do you mean we have to leave?' Fern demanded.

By the time the others joined him at the burrow entrance to the riverbank, Sylvan had settled on their course of action. But when he tried to explain it to them the argument started. Fern was in a terrible mood. Sylvan couldn't really blame her, he supposed, but didn't see that he really deserved

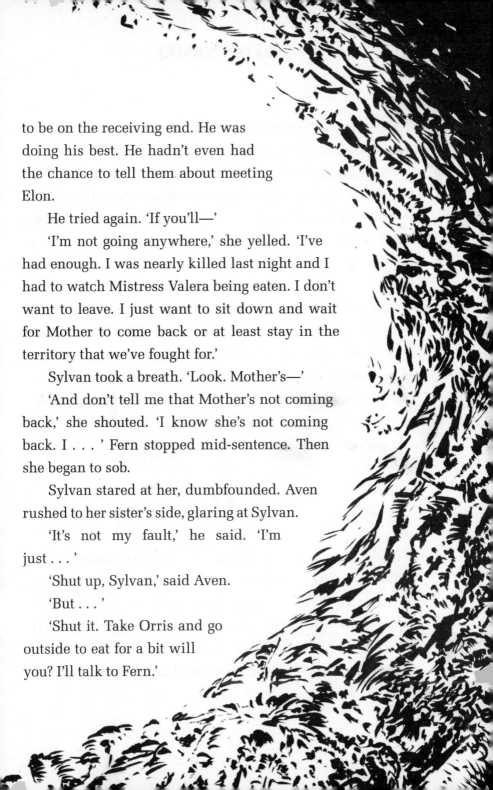

to be on the receiving end. He was
doing his best. He hadn't even had
the chance to tell them about meeting
Elon.

He tried again. 'If you'll—'

'I'm not going anywhere,' she yelled. 'I've
had enough. I was nearly killed last night and I
had to watch Mistress Valera being eaten. I don't
want to leave. I just want to sit down and wait
for Mother to come back or at least stay in the
territory that we've fought for.'

Sylvan took a breath. 'Look. Mother's—'

'And don't tell me that Mother's not coming
back,' she shouted. 'I know she's not coming
back. I . . . ' Fern stopped mid-sentence. Then
she began to sob.

Sylvan stared at her, dumbfounded. Aven
rushed to her sister's side, glaring at Sylvan.

'It's not my fault,' he said. 'I'm
just . . . '

'Shut up, Sylvan,' said Aven.

'But . . . '

'Shut it. Take Orris and go
outside to eat for a bit will
you? I'll talk to Fern.'

Sylvan and Orris exchanged glances. Orris rolled his eyes and gestured with his head and they quietly sloped off, leaving the girls to it. They stayed well under cover, feeding because they should, keeping a watchful eye on the sky.

After some time Orris said, 'Did you mean that about leaving?'

Sylvan nodded. 'Yes.'

'Oh.'

Orris munched on a stem of forget-me-not. Somewhere a heron cried, making them both tense. But it was far away and little threat. It was a while longer before Orris said, quietly, 'We're going to die, aren't we?'

Sylvan faced his brother. 'No, Orris, we're not. I'll tell you what we're going to do. We're all going to leave here. We're going to get away from this creature, whatever it is. We're going to stay together. We're going to find a new place where there are Singers and where the creatures can't find us. It'll be difficult but we'll be together and we'll all be just fine.'

Orris raised his head. 'You think so?'

'Definitely. Don't worry. I have it all worked out,' Sylvan lied. He wished he felt anything like as confident as he sounded. From behind them came the sound of a throat being cleared, meaningfully. Sylvan spun round to face Fern and Aven.

'It's all worked out, is it? That's nice to hear,' said Aven, drily.

'Erm—' Sylvan began. Aven over-rode him.

'Don't be shy, let's hear it.'

Sylvan glanced at Fern. 'Are you going to shout at me again?'

Fern shook her head. 'No. Sorry.'

'All right. I met someone this morning. He's a male called Elon. He told me some things.'

Sylvan recounted their conversation. When he was finished Fern said, 'I still don't see why this means we have to leave. I mean we've already escaped twice. And we don't even know if there are any other Singers, or whether there is anywhere else we can live. And even if there was, the whole bank could be filled with those creatures.'

Sylvan had no answer. He had no real plan, but only a growing certainty that leaving was the right thing to do.

Sinethis had made a pact with him, told him to flow with her. They should follow her downstream. The urge to go was like an ache in him, as if he was being tugged downflow by an unseen force. It wasn't a lot to go on, though. The others weren't going to leave just because he said they should.

'It's true we escaped,' he said, slowly. 'But we only survived because it got distracted by something bigger. I mean, last night it was Mistress Valera. The first time . . . '

Sylvan tailed off. Aven stared at him.

'You think we survived because we're too small to bother with?' she said.

Sylvan nodded. Aven looked horrified. 'So if things keep going we'll soon be the biggest Singers around. Even me. I don't know about you, but I don't want to go to nest every night wondering if it'll be the last time I do it.'

'But what if there's nothing else and this is the only place we've got? What if the whole of the Great River is full of these creatures?' said Orris.

'Then we'll be in trouble,' said Sylvan. 'But we're in trouble anyway. And if we leave we have a chance. Anything's got to be better than sitting here waiting to be taken. And I know it sounds weird, but I have a feeling that if we leave things will be OK.'

The four voles were silent. Eventually Fern said, 'So, assuming we decide to leave, which way do we go?'

They turned to Sylvan. 'Downflow, away from the creature,

through Mistress Valera's territory and on until we're safe.'

He could not explain it, but he was even more sure that it was right, that they needed to follow the Great River. He looked at his family. 'What do you say?'

For answer, Aven looked back at the entrance to the little burrow. She bowed her head and turned away, her back to Mistress Esther's empty territory and the spreading tree with its stench of the creature and its terrible memories. She began to walk. After an instant, Fern followed. Sylvan looked at his brother.

'Orris?'

'All right. Let's try.'

Sylvan smiled. 'Good vole. It'll be fine. You'll see.'

'I doubt it.'

They fell into file behind the girls, making their way through the grasses and on down towards Mistress Valera's territory. Despite everything Sylvan felt his heart lift a little. When they had woken that morning they had been four frightened vole pups, alone and directionless. Now they were following Sinethis. They had a purpose.

PART 2
THE JOURNEY

They travelled all the first day, meeting a few Folk as they went. Mistress Valera's territory was scruffy and unkempt, and laced with her bitter scent. They passed through quickly, seeing no one.

At the border of her territory, they startled another female from feeding and she looked as though she might attack. She let them pass, though, when Aven pointed out that they were juveniles and couldn't do any harm. In exchange they told her about Mistress Valera. At the mention of the creature, she cast a fearful look back into her burrow and cut the conversation short before running back home, leaving them free to continue. Fern said that she might have pups in there and that she wouldn't want to be in her position, with a new litter and everything.

After that, there was nothing. No more females. The few males they encountered would not stop to talk, but hurried away, intent on their own business. The grasses were luxuriant and uncropped, and empty burrows stood in the banks. Yellowed grass stems from Singers' feeding littered the water's edge. Tiny plants grew in the bare earth runs. The boundary markers were disintegrating. Elon's warning had proved accurate: the Great River was being emptied of her Singers.

They found a burrow for the first night. They slept lightly, surrounded by the odours of past River Singers, and left early the next morning. This time as they journeyed, the Great River began to change around them. Beyond her, trees began to sprawl across the sky, blotting out the sun, growing thicker the further they went. By the time the evening shadows lengthened, they were in an alien world. The shade was dense and the banks cold and dark. The familiar grasses and herbs were reduced to tiny clumps where the branches let in enough light. The River Singers sheltered in these rare stands, feeding quickly, talking little, before dashing to the next across the bare earth and

low vegetation. Black crows crowded the trees, calling to one another in coarse voices that sent chills down Sylvan's spine. No burrows, no markers, no sign; only woods that looked as though they could continue for ever. And if they did, Sylvan thought, how would they survive? They were terribly exposed here. And now darkness was descending and they had no burrow for the night. They hurried on, scampering between meagre shelters, anxious and watchful. Finally, as the light had almost failed, Aven spotted an untidy heap of burrows set back from the water, protected by a narrow fringe of reeds. They stopped and stared up at the scruffy entrances.

'I don't like the look of it,' said Orris.

Sylvan bit back an angry response. Orris had been moaning ever since they left. It was beginning to get on his nerves.

'They're burrows, aren't they?'

Orris eyed them, suspiciously. 'Maybe. But they don't look right.'

He had a point, Sylvan had to concede. There were far more burrows than usual, linked with a series of dirty runs through a scatter of nettles. None of the entrances were in their proper places: none by the water, and no grazing holes. They were too large and the wrong shape. Outside lay discarded seed husks and stinking black droppings. And underlying everything was a strange scent; like a vole's smell, but different, more pointy. Sylvan cast an eye to the falling darkness.

'I don't really see that we have much choice,' he said. 'It's these or a night in the open.'

As if to accompany the thought a tawny owl hooted overhead, preparing for the night's hunt. Orris jumped. Sylvan turned to the others. 'What do you think?'

'I'm too tired to think,' said Aven.

'Not helpful.'

'I think that it's a shelter,' said Fern. 'And we need shelter.'

'Well I still don't like it,' said Orris. 'How do we know there isn't something in there already?'

'We don't, Orris,' said Sylvan. 'But we do know there are going to be things out here.'

'What if the things in there are nastier than the things out here?'

Sylvan lost his temper. 'I tell you what, then, I'll go first. That way, if I get eaten, at least you'll have the pleasure of knowing you were right. Before the owls and foxes get you.'

Orris started to speak but Sylvan cut him off. 'No, Orris, you're right. You wait here and I'll go in to investigate. That way at least some of us might survive.'

He began marching up towards the burrow entrance, ignoring the protests behind him. Even as he stamped up the slope Sylvan knew that he was being too hard on his brother. But he was also full of the injustice of the world, tired, scared, doing his best, and sick of Orris's whining. As he approached the first burrow, though, his anger cooled and, as if to fill the space, fear ran though him.

Up close, the strangeness of the burrows was clear. They smelt awful. The odour made him want to run and hide. He reached the lip of the nearest hole and peered into the gloom within, repulsed by the medley of scents emanating from it. He could see nothing. He listened intently. Nothing. Heart thumping, he risked a few steps up the tunnel. His paws echoed on dried mud. Nothing immediately ran to attack, and so he carried on inward, whiskers twitching. Here and there patches of the smell were stronger, but underpinned by more homely notes of damp soil and roots. His feet carried him to where, in a Singer's burrow, the nest should be. But here the layout was strange. All of the tunnels in their home burrow led to the Great River, running from the high nest chambers down to the water. Here the tunnels ran horizontally back into the bank, or parallel to the water's edge. This burrow treated Sinethis as if she were simply a part of the landscape, or worse, something to be avoided.

Deep inside now, Sylvan could see little. His whiskers brushed the walls and the pattern of scents carried him onward. He reached a fork in the passage and picked the uphill turn. A short tunnel quickly opened into a nest chamber. He eased himself inside. The walls were rough and badly maintained and along the ceiling was a large crack through which a dull twilight filtered. Two tunnels led into the chamber, opening side by side, one that he had come from and another that led off to who-knew-where. From the other tunnel the scents were stronger, more acrid. But, Sylvan thought, the chamber would do. He wouldn't be sorry to leave, but it was shelter.

He turned to fetch the others. As he did, Sylvan caught a movement from the corner of his eye. His head snapped

round. From the second tunnel a pair of eyes reflected grisly red. He jumped back, teeth bared, squeaking a challenge, flattening himself against the chamber wall. The only response was a dry chuckle. Yellow incisors flashed in the half-light.

'I hears it, I does.'

The voice was gravelly, the accent odd. It was the language of the Folk, but the words were garbled, unclear.

'I wonders what we has.'

'Wh-who are you?'

'It doesn't belong here, it doesn't. I knows it. I hears it. I smells it. What is it, I wonders?'

'What is it?' Sylvan asked. 'W-what do you mean?'

The stranger paused again. 'What is it in my home?'

'You want to know what I am?'

More chuckling from the darkness. 'Ah. Has brains it does. But not answering, methinks. I asks it for last time: what is it?'

Sylvan was cornered. He cursed himself for having jumped back into the chamber. Whatever this thing was, he would have to run past it to escape. Despite his racing heart and the fear pumping through him, a part of him was thinking hard. This creature was speaking to him. If it wanted to talk, perhaps it could be persuaded to leave him alone. Or at least to keep talking until the others arrived. If they ever did.

'I'm a River Singer,' said Sylvan, trying to keep his voice from shaking. 'One of the Folk.'

A pause. 'Ah. Understands, I does.' The darkness around

the stranger gave an impression of deep contemplation.
'I wonders, then: knows what I is, does it?'

'No, I don't know. Sorry.'

'Ah. Never seen one, has it? Likes to keep to itself? Tsk.
Not sociable.' More chuckling. 'I jokes, see?'

Sylvan tried to humour it. 'Yes. Good joke.'

The chuckling stopped.

'You jokes me too, methinks?'

'No, I don't mean to joke you,' said Sylvan, hurriedly.

Abruptly the stranger pattered forward. It was far, far
bigger than any water vole that Sylvan had ever seen. It looked
like a Singer, but horribly deformed. Its face was pointed and
its ears, rather than flat on its head, were rounded and erect.
Its fur was greyish brown and behind it a hairless tail whipped

the air. Sylvan shrank back as far as he could. It stopped a few paces away and regarded him, beadily. It gave off an air of sharp intelligence, at odds with its broken speech.

'Knows now, does you, what River Singers calls us?'

'No,' Sylvan squeaked.

'Thinks not. Calls us "rats",' it said. It put its head on one side. 'Knows me, does you?'

Oh no! A rat! Sylvan's mind flooded with the tales he had heard. Talkers, charmers, not to be trusted. Turn your back and they will fill your burrows, take your babies. They claim the Great River, breeding and crowding, driving the Folk from their homes. Rats. Bad news. Trouble.

And he was in its burrow.

The rat grinned, seeing the expression on Sylvan's face. 'Ah. Heh. I sees that you do. And you is River Singer. And you is small. And this—' The rat gestured at the nest chamber, 'is a rat home. Knows, does you, what happens when River Singers find themselves in rat homes?'

Sylvan, miserably frightened, shook his head. 'No.'

'Is good for one: rats or Singers. Knows which it is?'

Sylvan closed his eyes, briefly. 'Singers?' he ventured.

'Is wrong, that.' The rat's grin widened. 'But brains you has. Gives you another guess I does.'

Sylvan cast about him in mounting panic. No escape but the tunnel. He crouched, ready to make a desperate break for the river. Seeing this, the rat, too, tensed.

'Sylvan?' Aven's voice echoed up from the burrow entrance. The rat cocked an ear. Its grin disappeared. It gave Sylvan a searching look.

'Sylvan, is it?'

'Yes.'

'Has friends does you?'

'Yes, I do. Lots.'

'Ah. Mayhaps not be good for rats, then.'

'Sylvan!' Aven called again.

Sylvan eyed the giant rat in front of him. It was obviously considering its alternatives, faced with an unknown number of water voles outside. Sylvan squared his stance a little.

'I'd better reply,' he said. He did not add, *because otherwise they'll be scared*. The rat hesitated for interminable moments. Then it bowed its head and withdrew slowly backwards down its tunnel, keeping his eyes locked on Sylvan, submerging in the gloom until only its red eyeshine was visible. Sylvan could have sobbed with relief. It no longer blocked his exit.

'I'm here,' Sylvan called, fighting to keep his voice level. 'I'm coming out. Wait there.'

He stepped cautiously past the rat, keeping it within sight until he was safely past. He was about to run for it when the rat spoke.

'Fodur,' it said from the shadows.

'What?' said Sylvan, one leg raised.

'My name: Fodur.'

'Right,' said Sylvan. 'Fodur. Nice to meet you.'

Then he fled, scurrying as quickly as he could for the exit. Fodur's surprised chuckle followed him, echoing down the tunnel.

'So it's a straight choice between spending the night in there with the rats—'

'I only saw one rat.'

'Whatever. It's a choice between rat, or possible rats, and out here with the owls and foxes,' said Aven.

'Yes,' said Sylvan unhappily. 'That's the choice.'

'How did it smell in there?' asked Fern.

'What has that got to do with anything?'

'Well, you can tell a lot—'

'If you're about to say that you can tell a lot about a place from the smells, I'm going to bite you,' said Sylvan. 'It was a rat's home. It had a big rat living in it. How do you think it smelt?'

'I don't know,' said Fern, with infuriating calm. 'That's why I'm asking.'

'It—' Sylvan stopped and thought for a second. 'It smelt pretty bad. But once I was in it wasn't too strong. It smelt a bit empty, really. But I still nearly ended up in a fight with a massive rat.'

'Did you?' asked Fern.

'I told you, didn't I? Weren't you listening?'

'Yes,' said Fern, 'I was. I was also thinking, which you don't seem to have been.'

'Oh, I am sorry,' said Sylvan, bitterly. 'I was a bit busy trying to talk it out of attacking me. But I'm sure if I'd asked it to leave me alone for a bit, while I had a good think, it would have been reasonable about it.'

'Shut up, Sylvan,' Aven advised him.

Sylvan blinked. Fern continued, 'Thank you, Aven. It didn't attack you, and if it was as big as you say, it could have, easily. And it told you its name.'

'So?'

'So maybe it was trying to be friendly.'

'It wasn't doing a very good job.'

Fern gave him the look she reserved for utter morons. 'But it didn't attack you, did it? And you were in its home. What would happen if you had gone into a water vole burrow?'

'Don't know.'

'Oh, come on. Remember Mistress Valera? There would be a fight for sure. No talking, just a fight.'

'So what? I still don't think that spending a night with a potentially violent rat is a good idea.'

'Of course it isn't a good idea,' said Aven. 'It's a completely stupid idea. It's just that standing around in the open waiting to be eaten by a fox while you two discuss it is even more stupid.'

As she spoke, the owl called overhead, and a shadow drifted silently across the river. Orris squeaked and Fern glanced up, nervously. The darkness was coming on quickly. Sylvan, came to a decision. Not, he thought, that they had much choice. Outside meant death.

'All right,' he said. 'Let's get into the tunnel. Fern, we'll have to go up and talk to Fodur or whoever he is. Aven and Orris follow us in but stay near the exit. If there's any trouble at least you two can get out. OK?'

Sylvan turned without waiting for a response, and began grimly climbing back up the spoil heap to the burrow entrance. Fern hurried to catch him up.

'Why me?' she asked.

Sylvan kept walking. 'Well, you were so keen to meet the rat. Besides, I'll need someone with me to do the thinking while I'm busy panicking.'

Fern struggled to keep up. 'Are you trying to make a point?'

'No,' said Sylvan. 'But you did really well with Mistress Valera. I'll feel better with you there as a backup, that's all.'

'Oh,' said Fern, 'that's a really nice thing to say.'

Sylvan concentrated on picking his way past the refuse scattered across the slope, trying not to think about what lay inside. 'Don't get used to it.'

They reached the tunnel entrance. It looked dark and forbidding.

'Ready?' he asked.

Fern shook her head.

'Me neither.'

He called quietly to Aven and Orris to follow them up, then he walked up and into the darkness. The sound of Fern's paws on the earth floor behind him was reassuring.

'Fodur?' he shouted.

No response.

'Fodur?'

They waited. Nothing.

'Maybe he's left,' said Fern.

'I don't think so,' said Sylvan. He couldn't put his paw on it, but he had the feeling that Fodur was up there, still in the chamber. Something Fodur said had stuck in Sylvan's head. *Mayhaps not be good for rats, then.* As ridiculous as it sounded, Sylvan wondered if the rat was frightened of them.

Oh well. Only one way to find out.

'Mr Fodur. Can we come up? I promise it won't be bad for rats.'

Sylvan was grateful he couldn't see Fern's expression in the gloom. The words sounded stupid. Oddly, though, they seemed to work.

'Promises does you?' The words echoed down to them, carrying a hint of amusement, but a hint of something else, that might have been caution.

'Yes, I do. There are four of us. But only two coming up. The others are below. We want to talk.'

'Talk. Heh. What does it talk about, I wonders?'

'Does that mean we can come up?'

No answer.

'Please?'

The moments dragged out.

'Come, then.'

Sylvan took a breath. 'Right,' he muttered. 'Here goes.'

He set off for the chamber, Fern following. With each step he braced for an attack, almost able to see the flash of red eyes and feel the slash of teeth tearing at his flesh. If Fern had not been behind him he might have hesitated, but instead he kept on placing one foot before the next. Soon enough they were outside the chamber. As they approached, the rat's voice called out to them.

'You returns, then.'

Sylvan edged into the room. Fodur hunched in the centre, looking huge in the confined space. He stared at the Singers balefully.

'What is this other?'

Sylvan nudged Fern, who was staring at the rat.

'Oh, I'm Fern,' she said.

'A Singer is you?'

'Yes. I'm his sister.'

'Ah. Heh. Sees I does. And the others? Sisters?'

'One is,' said Sylvan. 'The other is my brother.'

'Male. Four Singers, two male. Wonders what they wants in rat burrow. Is mine, this. What do you wants?'

Sylvan hesitated. A wrong step now could be a disaster. Being chased by a rat through dark burrows and out into the night . . . Sylvan shivered. Fern spoke before he could find the words.

'We know it's yours, Mr Fodur. We only want to stay for the night. We'll be gone as soon as it's daylight.'

Fodur chuckled. 'Ah. Forgets I does. Singers not night runners. Dark is rat friend only. We sees, we runs, we eats. You sleeps. Is different, yes?' The chuckling stopped. 'But four Singers is many. You likes burrow. Mayhaps you thinks to stay. Bad for rats, methinks.'

'We really don't want to stay,' said Fern. 'We couldn't even if we did. It would be too dangerous.'

'Dangerous,' Fodur repeated, softly. 'Wonders why.'

'Because we had to leave our colony. Our mother was killed by a creature, one we have never seen before. Our neighbours are dead. So we left. But we can't stay here. There's nothing for us to eat, and even if there was, we'd be hunted by the creature. So in the morning we will go.'

There was no sound in the little black chamber but the rasp of Fodur's breathing. The moments stretched away and still he gave no response or sign that he had heard.

'Ah,' he said finally. His voice was sombre. The laughing note had gone. 'Creature. Sees I does. Thinks this bad for rats.'

Sylvan tensed. This was not going how he hoped. They might have to run, or worse fight their way down to the others. He fixed his gaze on Fodur, ready to flee at the first sign of danger. But Fodur said, 'I decides. You stay. This night you be rat friend and I be Singer friend. In the morning you leaves. You promises.'

Relief rushed through Sylvan.

'Thank you, Fodur,' he said. 'I promises . . . er . . . promise. In the morning we'll be gone.'

Fodur chuckled. 'Best you be. Rat burrows not good for Singers. Is word for it. "Unsanitary", thinks it is. Call your friends. Sleep. Fodur leaves now. Has night business.'

Without waiting for a response Fodur stood up and pattered briskly away down his tunnels. He was soon lost amidst the gloom and night noises.

Fern sidled closer to Sylvan. 'Well, it looks like we have a burrow for the night. The rat, though: can we trust it?'

Sylvan sighed. Suddenly he felt incredibly tired. 'Maybe. It's not like we have any choice anyway. Let's get the others up here.'

Sylvan went down to fetch Aven and Orris. Orris looked around him nervously as he entered the chamber, as if expecting an army of rats to flood out of the darkness and attack them. Aven surveyed the burrow with distaste.

'Well,' she said. 'This *is* nice, isn't it? Homely, in a rat-infested sort of a way.'

'It'll do for the night,' said Sylvan. 'Let's get some sleep.'

He curled up. He knew he should keep watch, make sure the others were all right, but now that they had somewhere, he found he could hardly keep his eyes open. The others settled around him, nestling together. He was asleep in moments.

The night was full of half-remembered dreams. Sylvan awoke in dim light filtering into the nest chamber. He had a hazy memory of Fodur staring at them in the darkness. He looked over at the sleeping forms of Fern and Aven, curled around one another. He blinked. He rubbed at his eyes. He turned his head the other way . . . and scrambled onto his feet with a gasp.

'F-Fodur. What are you doing?'

The rat was
squatting a couple
of paces from Sylvan,
staring intently at where
Sylvan had been sleeping. He
blinked and appeared to come to
himself.

'Ah. Sorry I is. Not mean to
frighten nice Singer.'

'I'm not frightened,' Sylvan lied, straightening
his ruffled fur. Fodur chuckled, fixing Sylvan with an
intelligent eye.

'Is not right, that.'

'Well, OK. You were staring a bit, though.'

'Ah. Heh. Not staring. Thinking. Bethinking me.'

Sylvan relaxed a little. 'You were bethinking you?'

'Yes.'

'What were you thinking?'

Out of the corner of his eye, Sylvan could see that
Fern and Aven had also woken and were listening
to the conversation. Orris was still fast asleep.

'Wonders why four Singers come to rat
place. Creature must be bad for Singers.
Worse than others. Was thinking I
knows it.'

Sylvan blinked. Fodur's speech was difficult to follow.

'Sorry, what do you know?'

'I knows it, the creature. They calls it "minks".'

'Mink?'

'Mink,' Fodur confirmed. 'We rats hears of it. Black, big, vicious. Not stoat, not weasel. Kill Singers. Kill rats. We knows it. We fears it.'

'Mink,' Aven repeated. When she said it the word sounded odd, as if saying it made the creature more substantial, somehow. More real. 'So it's got a name.'

'Mr Fodur,' said Fern, 'who is the "we" you keep talking about?'

Now Fern had asked, the question seemed obvious. Sylvan glanced around. They had chosen the burrow from necessity, but he realized they really had no idea how many more rats there might be.

'Ah. Singers not sociable. Not liking each other methinks. Rats is better. We knows things, finds things, pass things to others.'

'Are there more rats here, then?' asked Aven, glancing about.

The question had an unexpected effect on Fodur. He dropped his gaze to the floor. As difficult as it was for Sylvan to read rats' expressions, Sylvan sensed that the question had upset him.

'No,' said Fodur, quietly. 'I is with myself only.'

'Why?' blurted Aven.

In response Fodur ducked his head again. Fern gave Aven a disapproving look.

'Sorry,' said Aven.

'Never mind,' Sylvan cut in. 'We don't need to know. We just need to get going.'

Fodur's head came up. 'Is right, that. Away from rats, away from minks. Best for Singers.'

Sylvan smiled. Fodur wanted them to leave. He couldn't blame him.

'OK, let's wake Orris up, eat some food, and get going.' Sylvan turned to Fodur. 'Thank you for letting us stay here. It was nice of you to help us. Is it all right if we graze outside your burrow. You won't need the food?'

'Is not rat food, that. Singers eat what they wants.'

'Thank you. Come on, let's go.'

They woke Orris and trooped down through the tunnels to the small patch of reeds outside Fodur's burrow. As they left, Sylvan glanced back. Fodur was sitting perfectly still, gazing after them.

There was something creepy in the way he stared fixedly ahead. But the rat had let them stay the night and leave in the morning. That had to count for something. Sylvan concluded that he was probably just odd. And when they stepped cautiously out into the daylight, the whole encounter already seemed like part of yesterday's troubles.

After a breakfast of tough reed stems they set off along the tree-shaded banks, accompanied by cawing from the crows overhead. The noise was constant and uncomfortable. After a while it seemed to etch itself into their souls, making them nervy and irritable. As they dashed from cover to cover they cast constant fearful glances at the sky. They saw no more burrows, rat or otherwise, but on the soft mud beneath their feet were footprints, some rat-sized that could have belonged to Fodur, and some huge that tic-tacked along the water's edge, accompanied by an unmistakable sharp-sour smell.

'It's a fox,' said Fern. 'It must have come along here last night.'

They shared an unspoken vision of what would have happened if they had been caught in the open. Sylvan was even more grateful to the strange rat for letting them into his burrow. They had no idea what was ahead of them down the river. He wondered again if they were doing the right thing. But he thought of the Great River and her promise, and turned an ear to her gurgling flow. For an instant he felt an echo of the warm feeling he had experienced when they set off.

He strengthened his resolve. Somewhere downstream was a home for them, he was sure of it. It was his job to get them there. And he would.

'Fox, eh?' he replied with forced cheerfulness. 'Good thing we were in a burrow, then. Come on, let's get out from these trees and see if we can find somewhere decent to eat.'

It was early afternoon when Orris said that he thought that something was following them. Despite Sylvan's optimism, the trees had not only continued but become denser. They had found nowhere safe to sleep and had only been able to snatch occasional mouthfuls of some bitter herbs as they walked. They were tired, irritable, and hungry and Sylvan was worried. Things were not looking good. And now this.

'Are you sure?' he asked.

Orris nodded. 'I keep hearing it.'

'Keep hearing what, exactly?' asked Aven.

Orris shook his head. 'Don't know. It keeps stopping and starting. I don't like it, though.'

'Oh, great,' said Sylvan. He surveyed the bare riverbanks. No cover, just scattered, short plants. They were pathetically vulnerable. He listened intently for any sounds behind them. Right at the edge of hearing there was a brief rustle. Then

nothing. Another rustle, louder this time. The voles tensed, all of them facing back the way they had come, ready to fight or run. Another rustle, and something large and grey, still partly hidden by plants, scampered forwards a few paces, hunched close to the ground. It came through a patch of nettles, making the leaves shake. It left the nettles and scurried forward with surprising speed, giving Sylvan his first good look. He let out a breath. It wasn't going to eat them. It was Fodur.

The rat pattered closer, stopping a short distance away from the voles. The sight of him made Sylvan uneasy. He was out of breath and wild-eyed.

'Fodur, what are you doing here?'

'Is good, is good. Find Singers I does,' he panted.

'Yes but what I want to know is *why* did you find them?'

'Bethinks me,' said Fodur. 'Wants to come with Singers. Can help.'

Sylvan stared. 'Why?'

Before Fodur could answer, the air filled with the sound of flapping wings as crows took flight from the trees overhead, spooked by something. They circled and settled once more, cawing noisily from one to the other.

The Singers shrank back into the scant cover until the wings were still.

Fern said, 'I don't think this is the best place for a discussion.'

'She's right,' said Aven. 'As long as there's nothing chasing Fodur, I reckon the rest can wait.'

'No chasings for Fodur,' said Fodur. 'But things he must tell Singers. Important things.'

'Like what?' asked Sylvan.

'Ahead here is ratpatch. Many rats,' said Fodur.

Sylvan's heart sank. 'How many?'

'Many, many. Bad for Singers. But mayhaps Fodur helpful. Could be Singer friend. Could help with ratpatch.'

Sylvan was filled with misgivings, but the five of them could not sit on the riverbank without expecting trouble. And if there were more rats ahead the trouble could be a lot worse. He nodded, reluctantly.

'OK. But if you come with us we're going to need answers later.'

Fodur nodded. 'Promises, I does.'

'I suppose that's good enough.'

'But—' began Orris, looking unhappily at Fodur.

Sylvan cut him off. 'His promise was good enough last night when we needed it. It should be good enough now. Right?'

Orris dropped his gaze and nodded.

'Right then. Fodur, you'd better go first. If there are rats ahead then you'll be able to talk to them for us.' *And*, Sylvan added in the privacy of his own head, *that way we'll be able to keep an eye on you.*

The rat set off. Sylvan motioned for Orris to go ahead. Orris looked unhappy but did not argue. Sylvan fell back alongside Aven and Fern, and the three of them walked along in a tight group.

'What do you think?' he whispered.

'I thought you just said his promise was good enough,' said Aven.

'I know what I said,' said Sylvan. 'I just don't know if I was right.'

'Well, I'm not ecstatic about following a strange rat into unfamiliar territory, if that's what you mean.'

'Neither am I. I have a feeling there's going to be trouble,' said Fern.

Sylvan agreed. Fodur had not been dangerous so far, but why did he want to travel with four River Singers? What did he have to gain? And if they were wrong, and if Fodur was a danger, it could turn out very badly for them. But then everything could turn out badly anyway. They needed all the help they could get, and Fodur sounded as if he knew the area. Still, he wouldn't make the mistake of trusting the rat too far. Not yet. He put the questions to one side and concentrated on watching for danger.

Ahead, Fodur gave a cry of surprise. Abruptly the voles and Fodur were surrounded by rats, chattering at one another in strange accents, laughing, shoving, and running all around the group, jumping and squeaking. These rats were smaller than Fodur, not much bigger than Sylvan. One of them, larger than the rest, plonked itself in front of Fodur. The others fell into something resembling order behind it, still jostling.

'Whatzitwhatzit?' demanded the rat. The other rats went quiet, listening for Fodur's response.

'Israts, knowzit yedoes,' said Fodur.

'Noknows, notrats. Whatzitwhatzit?' demanded the spokes-rat, pointing at Sylvan.

'Israts, Izez. Meanz'ee nosayme?'

'Hahsez . . . ' began the spokesrat, but the rest of its reply

made no sense to Sylvan. Fodur's response too was almost impossible to follow. Some of the words were familiar, but for all he understood the rats could have been speaking another language. Sylvan realized that when Fodur had spoken to them he must have been trying to be easy to understand. At one point Fodur pointed at him, and identifiable noises emerged from the gibberish of the rat talk.

' . . . Sylvan . . . '

Before Sylvan could move or speak, another rat dropped in front of him, making him jump.

'Sylvan is?'

'Erm, yes.'

'Speakzod, speakzod,' it called out. It shoved its head forwards, aggressively, twisted its neck around and pulled a funny face, tongue lolling out, eyes swivelling. Then it snapped back to seriousness. 'Fearszou makezit?' it asked.

'What?'

'Fearzou makezit? Doezitdoezit?'

'OK.'

The rat grinned and ran off, shouting, 'Fearzmefearzmefearzme.'

Sylvan looked round at the others. Aven was half amused, Fern looked alarmed. Orris, though, had one ear cocked, an expression of intent concentration on his face. Sylvan would have expected him to have curled into a ball by now, faced with this many rampaging rats. He sidled over to his brother.

'You OK?'

'Shhh. I'm listening.'

'What to?'

Impatience flitted across Orris's face. 'The rats,' he said.

'Why? I can't understand any of it,' said Sylvan.

'Can't you?'

'Can you?'

'Course. It's easy.' Sylvan blinked. Aven and Fern too gave Orris a surprised look.

Sylvan looked at his brother with new-found respect. 'OK, so what are they talking about?'

'I can't hear if you keep talking to me.'

Sylvan withdrew a couple of steps and waited for the rats' conversation to stop. After a pause Orris said, 'Well, Fodur told them that we're a group of travelling rats. They didn't believe him, said we looked weird.'

'Hah, they can talk,' muttered Aven.

Orris continued, 'Then Fodur said some stuff I didn't understand, but I think he told them that we're his children.'

Sylvan looked over at Fodur, who was still in negotiation. *Why would he say we're his children?* he thought. *Or that we're rats, for that matter?* Beyond Fodur, the other rats had found a snail and were attempting to push it down the hill into the water. Sylvan shook his head. Rats were weird.

'What did the rat say to that?'

'It said that we're ugly kids.'

Fodur and the spokesrat stopped speaking. They touched noses and the rat squeaked loudly at the others. In seconds, all of them had swarmed back into their burrows. Fodur limped back over to the voles, looking worried.

'What did they say? Were those important rats?' asked Sylvan.

'They's young ratlings. They know-nothings. But we needs to be moving.'

'But what did they say?' asked Fern.

Fodur shook his head. 'Not much. But this big ratpatch. Bad for Singers, thinks. Bad for Fodur. Best we's not here.'

'Why? They seem friendly enough,' said Sylvan.

Fodur looked agitated. 'Is truth, but we needs to move. Now.'

'OK,' said Sylvan. 'I won't argue. Let's go.'

'Fast, fast,' added Fodur, glancing at the burrow into which the young rats had disappeared.

'Right. "Fast, fast" it is. You lead.'

Fodur set off at a dead run. The voles could barely keep up with him. After their travels, Sylvan's legs were already aching, but Fodur left no time for them to catch their breath, pressing on down the riverbank. He dodged across open

ground as if predators did not exist. Sylvan could hear Orris behind him complaining. He shouted after Fodur to slow down, but the rat seemed not to hear him; if anything he ran harder. They had no option but to put their heads down and force their legs to work faster. Time passed in a hot, aching blur. As they ran, the trees overhead grew sparser, and the grasses longer. The banks here teemed with holes, but they were rat burrows. They fled past these, and on until the burrows became less numerous. At last Fodur stumbled to a halt. Sylvan staggered up behind him, head spinning and legs wobbling. He kept himself upright just long enough to ensure that the others had kept up and were safe, and then he collapsed, panting, into the lengthening shadows in a small patch of grass. Meanwhile Fodur was busy, sniffing carefully around the entrance to a burrow and running a little way up and down the tunnel before finally slumping into some long grass at the entrance.

'Mind . . . telling . . . me . . . what . . . that was . . . about?' panted Sylvan.

The rat's sides were heaving so hard that he could hardly speak. 'Ratpatch . . . Dangerous, dangerous . . . Safe here.'

'But this . . . this is also a rat . . . burrow,' said Fern.

'Is right, that . . . but not ratpatch,' said Fodur. 'Is empty. Knows it.'

Sylvan rolled painfully to his feet and nosed around the burrow entrance. It smelt faintly of rats, and of spiders and abandonment. He glanced at the falling daylight and the Great River. By the burrow her flow was relatively calm, but further down she became swift, turbulent, and unwelcoming. She would do for an escape, but it could be dangerous. He looked back at the burrow.

'OK. Let's get inside and safe and then you can tell us what's going on.'

They entered the disused burrow and threw themselves down in the first chamber they came to. It was musty but dry.

There were two entrances; one they had just come up and another that disappeared into the bank. Sylvan closed his eyes, trying to form an impression of the day they had just had. So many things had happened so quickly that he found it difficult to put them in order.

'Fodur,' he said, 'it's time for you to explain some things.'

Fodur nodded. 'Will,' he said.

From behind Sylvan Fern said, 'Let's start with the easy ones. Why were you so scared of those other rats? I thought you said rats were sociable?'

Fodur put his head on the side. 'Is sociable, yes. But rats has family. Singers have family, but family is small, yes? You not be liking unfamily Singers?'

Sylvan remembered Mistress Valera. 'Not much, no,' he said.

'Rats is same. But rat family is more rats than you can count. Many, many in ratpack. And ratpack not be liking unfamily rats.'

'Those others didn't seem so bad,' said Aven.

'Hah. Ratlings is know-nothings, they's fine. They play. They like fun, fun. But if they go to big bossrat . . . he not be liking Fodur. Not be liking Singers. We's not family rats.'

Fodur shuddered. 'Bad to fight ratpack. I knows this. All ratpack chase us. Big fight. Much blood. Not good.'

Sylvan stared at Fodur, full of visions of being chased down the riverbank by packs of bloodthirsty rats.

'OK,' said Sylvan. 'I'm glad we ran. Thanks.'

'Not problem. More questions?'

'Why did you tell them we were your children,' asked Orris.

Fodur chuckled. 'Good wheeze, that. Fooled ratlings, yes?'

'Erm, yes. I suppose,' said Sylvan, 'But why?'

'You not know-nothing. Has brains. You bethinks you.'

Sylvan blinked stupidly. It was Fern who supplied the reason. 'They got bored with us because they thought we were rats. If they had thought we were River Singers they wouldn't have left us alone, would they? Then we would have been stuck until the adults turned up.'

'And that,' finished Aven, 'wouldn't have been pretty.'

Fodur nodded once, smiling encouragingly. 'Is right, that.'

Sylvan was impressed. 'So you got us out of trouble?'

Fodur nodded.

'I've got another question,' said Fern. 'It's not that we're not grateful, but why are you here? Why with us?'

An awkward silence filled the burrow. 'Afears me,' said Fodur eventually.

'You're frightened?' asked Aven. Fodur nodded. 'What of?'

'Minks.'

'Well I can see why,' said Sylvan. 'I mean that's why we're here. But isn't it different for rats? I can't imagine a mink going into a rat burrow. Too many rats in there . . . Oh.'

Sylvan tailed off. 'Yes,' said Fodur. 'Fodur by ownself. Fodur old, has no ratpatch, no family. All gone. Hoping if Fodur help Singers, mayhaps Singers help Fodur.'

'Perhaps,' said Sylvan.

'What happened to your family?' Aven cut in.

Fodur shook his head, obviously distressed. Aven looked embarrassed. 'Sorry,' she said. 'I keep doing that, don't I? I didn't mean to—'

'Is OK,' said Fodur quickly, looking up. 'Needs you know. We's driven from home. Find new place, new family. But then minks . . . none left.'

They didn't need to ask what had happened to the others. Sylvan felt his heart go out to the rat. Despite their differences, they had the same problem.

Sylvan cleared his throat awkwardly. 'We're going downflow. If you are going that way, then you can come with us.

OK?'

This last was directed at Aven, Fern, and Orris, who all nodded. Fodur blinked rapidly several times and nodded his head too.

'Thanks you,' he whispered. He sat up on his haunches and groomed his ears and whiskers for some moments, like Fern did when she was upset. When he had finished he fell back to all fours.

'Mayhaps I helps. Knows what ratlings call this place?'

Sylvan shrugged.

'Is Sinnerzurrunslun.'

Orris's lips moved as he worked it out. ' "Land surrounded by Singers",' he said.

Fodur nodded approvingly. 'Is right that.'

'Surrounded,' said Fern. 'Does that mean there are more Singers downflow?'

'Mayhaps,' said Fodur. 'Ratnames often true. But rats not think only of river. "Zurrun" mean all sides.'

'I don't understand,' said Sylvan.

'I think he means that "surrounded" doesn't only mean up and downflow, but also to either side of the river,' said Fern.

'Is right.'

'But that makes no sense,' Fern continued. 'Singers live on the Great River. That's our place. Away from the water all there is are woods and fields and enemies. There can't be Singers to either side. So it must mean downflow.'

'Mayhaps, but not right, thinks.'

'It'd be good to know, though,' said Sylvan.

'I wonder,' said Orris slowly, 'if the other rats know about the Singers. You know, the rats back there. They might know where to find them.'

Aven gave him a look. 'You mean the ones we just ran away from because they're incredibly dangerous?'

'Just asking,' said Orris. 'Would they?'

'Mayhaps,' said Fodur, looking uncertain. 'But not thinking is good idea to be asking them.'

'I agree,' said Sylvan. 'Look, thanks to Fodur we know there are more Singers around and that's great news. If there are Singers there will be food and shelter. And maybe we've got far enough from the mink, now. We don't need to risk anything else.'

'But what if they're not downstream,' protested Orris. 'What if they're away from the Great River like Fodur said?'

'And what,' said Aven, 'if you get your nose gnawed off by a rat who doesn't want to answer your questions?'

'Exactly,' said Sylvan. 'Tomorrow we'll head downflow and go and look for these other Singers.'

'But—'

'No, Orris,' said Sylvan, firmly. 'It's not a good idea.'

As the sun set they went out to feed. They offered Fodur some grasses but he refused with a chuckle, and went off to hunt for his own food. Sylvan glanced round, checking on the others. Fern and Aven looked happier than they had for some time. Orris was off to one side, talking with Fodur. Sylvan couldn't hear what they said, but Fodur's expression was grave. He was not sure why, but the sight made him uncomfortable. Still, he thought, the rat had proved himself more than useful today. And tomorrow they could set out with a new hope. Perhaps everything really was going to be all right.

'Sylvan. Sylvan, wake up.'

'Mmmm?'

'Wake up, will you?' Aven pawed urgently at his shoulder.

'Wha? Whasa maddur?'

'Orris is gone.'

His eyes snapped open. 'What?'

'I said Orris is gone. He isn't here.'

Sylvan came fully awake, heart pounding. 'How long has he been missing?'

'I don't know.'

Fern, now awake next to Sylvan said, 'Well, he might have gone out on his own for a bit.'

Sylvan was incredulous. 'Orris? Go out on his own? To where?'

'I don't know,' said Fern. 'I just don't think that panicking is going to help, that's all.'

'I'm not panicking. I'm worried,' snapped Sylvan.

'Where's Fodur?' asked Fern.

'I don't know,' said Aven. 'He left during the night. But I didn't think anything about it.'

'Do you think—' began Fern, but Sylvan wasn't listening. A sick sensation grew in the pit of his stomach. Orris and Fodur were missing. It could be coincidence but he didn't think so. He shouldn't have trusted the rat. He knew he should have been more careful. He rushed to the left most tunnel entrance.

'Orris!' he yelled. No response. 'Orris!'

His cries were cut short by Aven cuffing him with a paw.

'Ouch, what are you—'

'Quiet. We're in a rat burrow, Sylvan. We have no idea what's out there. Stop being a moron.'

'And start thinking, for Sinethis's sake,' added Fern. 'Let's just calm down and think for a moment.'

Sylvan glared at the pair of them. He forced himself to swallow his anger, and allow himself to breathe. 'Fine. What do you *think*, then?'

He never heard what Fern thought. From down the right-hand tunnel came the sound of irregular, scrabbling paws. Before they could react, Fodur burst into the chamber and staggered to a stop.

'I hears noises. What is they?'

Fern and Aven instinctively shrank back, but Sylvan was incensed. 'Like you don't know,' he said. 'Where's Orris?'

Fodur blinked. 'Orris not here?' He glanced from vole to vole.

'No, not here,' said Fern.

Fodur's expression was instantly one of distress. He moved his head from side to side. 'Not good, this. Stays here you should. I finds him. I returns.'

Fodur whipped around and sprinted away. He left a stunned silence in his wake.

'That sounds bad,' said Fern.

'Really? You think so?' said Sylvan, bitterly.

'Yes,' said Fern. 'I do. And if you think that having a go at me is going to help, then go ahead.'

'All right, so what would *you* do.'

'I don't know.'

'So we don't know anything,' said Sylvan. 'Well, I'm going to find out.' He made to leave.

'Fodur said to stay here,' said Fern. 'It might be dangerous.'

Even as she spoke, a terrible cry echoed up the tunnels followed by squeaking, scratching, and pattering. Sylvan hesitated, desperately wanting to do something, anything. But the sounds grew louder, paws on tunnels scurrying here and there and high-pitched squeaking—whether in anger or pain they could not tell—that came closer until it seemed that an entire colony of rats must be about to crash into their chamber. Sylvan backed away until he was level with a tunnel leading back to the water. He glanced down it then gestured to the other two, raising his voice over the clamour.

'Whatever happens, I want you to run for it down here. Get to the Great River and swim for the far side.'

'And what are *you* going to do?' asked Aven.

'I'll be running as fast as I can behind you.'

An ear-splitting yell sounded from just outside and a brown furry shape hurtled into the chamber. It was Orris, breathing hard but unhurt. He stumbled to a stop and stared wide-eyed around him.

'What are you still doing in here?' he yelled. 'Move!'

'But—'

'Run!' Orris grabbed for Fern and tried to shove her down the tunnel. 'Run now!' he yelled. She stared at him stupidly.

'Run, you idiots!'

Then Orris dashed past Sylvan and disappeared down the other tunnel. They looked at each other. Then all four of them hurtled downhill, sprinting crazily for the Great River. Behind him, the tunnel filled with the sound of feet, noises piling haphazardly up into the small nest chamber, spilling over, finding the tunnel and pursuing them down to the water's edge.

Orris burst into the daylight and dived headlong into the Great River. He hit the surface and was gone from view. Fern and Aven hit the water moments behind him. Even as the circle of daylight rushed towards Sylvan the sounds of pursuit grew louder. He dared not look back, but put his head down and willed his legs faster, chest heaving. Soil and vegetation scattered from beneath him and daylight flooded around him, searing his eyes. He stumbled to the bank edge and leapt. The water closed over him and he scythed downwards, twisting to the bottom, throwing up a cloud of sediment in his wake. And then all was quiet and cool, and he was pulling himself across the river with long strokes, bubbles streaming out behind him. He slid smoothly between the plants on the river floor, and tiny silver fish scattered before him. He swam until the wall of the opposite bank rose up before him. Then he headed up and ever-so-gently breached the water's surface in the lee of a tiny stand of reed. He pulled himself cautiously from the water and turned to face the far bank where, moments before, he had leapt into the Great River.

On the far shore rats were swarming excitedly up and down. They seemed to be looking at something, nudging one another and pointing. Amidst the chaos one rat stood apart. Even at this distance it looked huge, and Sylvan could see that the others were treating it with respect. It squeaked an order and the milling rats instantly obeyed, dashing further down the bank. This, thought Sylvan, must be the boss-rat Fodur had spoken of. He instinctively shrank further from its view. He watched until he was certain that the rats were not going to swim across. Only then did he go to find the others, easing his way through the plants on the bank, keeping a wary eye out for signs of pursuit. It did not take him long; Orris and the girls were standing in a tense group a little way down. He joined them.

'Well, that was fun, wasn't it? Did you see that big rat?'

They did not respond. Like the rats they were staring fixedly at a point on the river surface.

'What's going on?'

Fern pointed with her chin. 'Rat,' she said. 'And it's heading this way.'

Sylvan strained his eyes. He could just make out a rat's pointy face bobbing on the water's surface a long way from their side of the river.

'I don't reckon it'll be a problem,' said Aven. 'It's not what you'd call a natural swimmer.'

She was right. The rat was struggling to keep its head above the water, drifting downstream on the current. Even as they watched it, floated out of the calm water and was plucked into a stronger current. Sinethis had hold of it and was bearing it away, piling waves over its head. It went under and emerged, spluttering. On the far 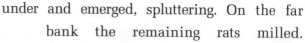 bank the remaining rats milled.

They had evidently decided that swimming was too much effort. It's strange, thought Sylvan. It didn't seem right, somehow, that one would be swimming across alone unless . . .

'Oh no,' said Orris. 'It's Fodur.'

Sylvan blinked, straining to make out the rat's features as it was carried further from them. Orris took a couple of steps towards the water and then paced backwards, dancing in an agony of indecision.

'What are you doing?' asked Sylvan.

Orris turned to face him. 'We have to help him,' he squeaked.

'But he—' Sylvan began but Orris cut him off.

'It's our fault . . . he needs us.' Orris stared imploringly at his brother. 'Help him. Please?'

'You can swim, can't you?'

Orris stared miserably downstream at the swiftly moving water. 'It's too fast,' he said. 'I can't do it. I can't swim like you. Help him.'

'Oh for Sinethis's sake,' said Aven. 'Come on, Sylvan.'

She dived into the water. In seconds the current took her, whisking her downstream until she was a tiny shape, carving a course down towards Fodur. Sylvan closed his eyes briefly. He was probably going to regret this.

'Keep up with us,' he ordered, and dived after Aven. Sylvan was bigger and a better swimmer but Aven had a head start. It was a colossal effort to catch her. He neared the swift water and Sinethis's flow took him, buffeting him on all sides and hurling him downflow. He gasped and swam harder, fighting against Sinethis's strength. He gained on Aven who was also swimming with grim determination. Further still, he could barely make out the tiny sight of Fodur, his head bobbing and swirling in the flow. They swam hard, keeping their heads up and their noses clear as the waters broke over them, spun them, or dragged at their legs. They closed on Fodur. The rat was in trouble, Sylvan could see, almost clawing at the water in his desperation to stay afloat. Wave after wave crashed over him, until his breath bubbled around his mouth. A side current smashed against him, threatening to overturn him. He clearly could not last. Sylvan and Aven, paddling frantically, drew close enough to hear Fodur's spluttering calls.

'Please,' he gasped. 'Please.'

'Hang on,' Sylvan yelled. 'We're coming.'

The Great River swept them round a corner, all white peaks and treacherous currents. Sylvan and Aven rode her flow as it brought them alongside the thrashing rat. Sylvan swam around Fodur's downflow flank, yelling at

Aven to get to the other side. She obeyed so that all three now swam side by side. Sylvan shoved upflow, stalling their downstream progress. Fodur's eyes were desperate, but Sylvan concentrated on getting them safe. Each moment carried them all further down. They needed to get to the side. Fodur was panting hard and his movements were jerky. Even flanked by the voles he could barely keep his head up. Any longer and he would drown.

Sylvan shouted over the river noise. 'That tree.'

Ahead was an immense tree with roots that spread down into the water. The flow swirled around the roots, forming a back eddy. If they could reach that, the water would be almost still. They began to steer the rat towards the relative calm. But Fodur was exhausted. His eyes were almost closed, and even as they swam his body began slip beneath the surface. He would not make it. He was going under.

'Squeeze him,' gasped Aven.

'What?'

'Squeeze him.'

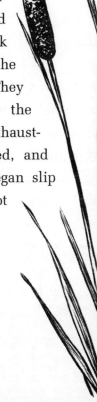

Sylvan saw what she meant. If they pressed into Fodur's sides they could take some of his weight. But as they pressed, Fodur gave a sharp cry, threw back his head, and breathed in water. With a hacking cough he was gone. Without thinking, Sylvan dived beneath him and shoved up, pushing the rat towards the air. Fodur breached the surface, spitting out water and inhaling a shuddering breath. Sylvan popped up beside him.

'What is it?' Sylvan shouted. 'What hurts?'

'Leg,' Fodur gasped. 'Back leg.'

'I'll push from the front. Aven? Ready?'

'Ready.'

Sylvan tried again, shoving in towards Fodur's flank. Aven did the same on the other side. Sylvan felt himself being borne down by the rat's weight. Aven was too small to take much of the burden, but between them it was enough. It was hard, awkward work. Sylvan's muscles ached and his lungs burned for air. But they were nearly at the eddy. A rustle in the reeds by the tree announced Orris's arrival. He staggered to a stop, breathing hard, at the edge of the bank.

'Get in here and help,' Aven yelled. 'He's too big.'

THE JOURNEY

Orris hesitated, but then leapt in and swam to them. He was only just in time. Fodur, final reserves spent, rolled over with a despairing cry. Aven was thrust under the surface and forced to kick away. She bobbed up, spluttering, a short distance away. Orris lunged, shoving powerfully against the rat's flank. Sylvan felt his own load lighten and between them they struggled into the shelter of the roots.

'The beach,' panted Sylvan, indicating a small shore of sandy earth, protected by two jutting roots. They made for it, feeling the water shallowing around them until their feet churned silt and contacted with firm mud. Chests heaving, they shoved and pulled at Fodur until all three of them collapsed on the riverbank. Aven swam up behind and hauled herself out. She threw herself down next to where Sylvan lay on his side, trying to recover his breath.

None of them spoke for a long moment. Sylvan raised his head.

'Everyone OK?'

'You mean apart from nearly drowning under a rat?' said Aven.

'I'll take that as a "yes". Orris?'

'I'm OK.'

He didn't sound OK. But there would be time for that later.

'How are you doing, Fodur?' No response. 'Fodur?'

Sylvan rolled to his feet. The rat was stretched out on his belly, eyes closed, ears flat. He looked as though he had drowned. He barely seemed to be breathing and blood was welling thickly from a large wound on his rear leg. The wound looked as if it had come from a rat bite. Something within Sylvan tightened. It was serious.

'This is bad. Very bad.'

Orris was quickly at Sylvan's side. 'Oh, no.'

'Yes,' said Sylvan. 'We have to get him under cover.'

Sylvan scanned the bank looking for a refuge, anywhere they could shelter.

'How about that?' asked Aven, pointing at a dark hole, leading back into the trunk of the tree. It was shelter of sorts, but it looked anything but inviting.

'Wait here,' said Sylvan. 'I'll check it out.'

He approached the hole cautiously, ready to dash for the water. He sniffed around the entrance. The scents were old. He sidled up to the door and ducked inside. Nothing but a floor of wood shavings that had rotted down to a dry powder. It was almost cosy.

He returned to the others. Fodur's eyes were open and

looked as though he was trying to speak. His mouth opened and shut but no words came out. Orris turned to Sylvan with a stricken face.

'Right,' said Sylvan. 'If we can get him in there, it's dry and warm.' He turned to Fodur. 'Can you walk?'

For answer, Fodur raised his head and nodded once. Then he slumped back down, eyes half shut.

'That's good, then,' said Sylvan, trying to sound cheerful. 'We'll help. Orris, Aven: same as in the water.'

The rat, scarcely conscious, manoeuvred his three un-injured legs beneath his body. He shoved himself upright and as soon as he was almost standing, Sylvan, Aven, and Orris bunched in against his flanks, supporting him. Together they wobbled their way into the comparative safety of the tree and dumped Fodur as gently as possible onto a pile of soft wood in the corner. He lay there, motionless. Sylvan gestured to the others and they withdrew a short distance.

'OK,' said Sylvan when they were out of earshot. 'Looks like we have an injured rat to look after. Are you OK to keep an eye on him if I go and find Fern?'

Orris nodded.

'And when I get back, is there any chance that you might explain why we've just been chased out of a burrow by a pack of rats?' Orris lowered his gaze, and nodded again. 'Good. Just so long as I know. I'll be back soon.'

It didn't take long to find Fern. She was picking her way down the Great River, keeping to the plants and out of sight. She told him that the rats had lost interest the second Fodur and the voles had been swept from view. The big rat had ordered them back to their burrows. That, at least, was a relief, thought Sylvan. He didn't fancy any more rat business today. He led Fern back to the tree where Fodur lay face

down, with eyes closed, barely breathing. Orris was sitting beside him, looking distraught and helpless. Aven was grooming herself dry off to one side. The voles foraged outside for some warm-looking leaves and moss, and piled these around Fodur. The rat did not respond. Sylvan examined him. Apart from the wound on his leg he was unhurt. But the wound looked terrible, red and gaping. Blood still welled from it, but more slowly than before. He turned to Orris.

'So,' he said, 'we've had a nice morning. How was yours?'

'I'm sorry,' Orris mumbled. 'I didn't mean for anyone to get hurt.'

'So this *is* your fault,' said Aven. There was an odd note in her voice. Shrill and un-Aven like. Orris nodded.

'So why don't you explain what happened?' said Sylvan. 'And make it simple for those of us who weren't expecting to have to run for our lives before breakfast.'

Orris looked miserable. 'Well Fodur said that the other rats might know something about the Singers nearby. And what he was saying about the word Sinnerzurrunslun made sense, you know about Singers in the fields, and I couldn't sleep and Fodur was awake so I . . . '

Orris tailed off and looked down at the slumped form of the rat. He swallowed. 'So I got Fodur to go back and ask the rats for more information.'

'You did *what*?' said Aven. 'Have you gone completely nuts?'

'You don't have to shout at me.'

'Yes I do,' shouted Aven. 'You nearly got us killed.'

Sylvan said, 'Come on, Aven. Let him speak.'

Aven subsided, glowering. Sylvan looked back at Orris. 'Go on,' he said.

'He didn't want to go back, said it'd be too dangerous. But I told him that all we needed to know was whether or not there were Singers off the Great River and maybe the ratlings might know. So he agreed. I said I'd go along to help, but he said that I'd only cause trouble . . . '

Sylvan stopped listening, his gaze resting on Fodur. Fodur had risked his life for them. A sick guilt settled in Sylvan's stomach when he thought that he had shouted at the rat, not trusted him, thought he had done something horrible; when instead it had been Orris who had put Fodur in danger. He forced his attention back.

' . . . when Fodur didn't get back I thought he must have been hurt or something. So I went out to see if I could find him. There were rats everywhere, and one of them found me and I ran and all of the rats started chasing me . . . ' Orris drew a shuddering breath. 'I ran and ran, but there were so many of them. I thought they were going to get me but Fodur jumped out of nowhere and started fighting the lead rat. I didn't see what happened after that, I was too busy trying to warn you . . . ' Orris closed his eyes. 'So Fodur's hurt and it's all my fault.'

None of the voles spoke for a while, but stared down at Fodur's inert body. Then Fern said, 'Fodur came back to the burrow while you were gone. He went back out to find you.'

'How could you be so stupid?' said Aven.

'It's done now, Aven—' Sylvan began but his sister rounded on him.

'No, Sylvan, it was stupid and he shouldn't have done it,' she yelled. Again there was something odd in her tone, something brittle.

'Aven, are you all right?'

For a second he thought she was going to yell at him again. But an instant later the anger drained from her and she sat down on the floor of the hollow.

'You know what?' she said. 'I'm not. I've had enough. All I want is to be somewhere safe with some nice grass and a warm burrow. Instead everything's horrible. Mother's dead, Orris could have been killed, and Fodur's hurt. We're a long way from home, we don't know where we're going, and we're running away from a mink. Even if we do find a new place to live, how do we know that it won't just be overrun by mink the second we get there? Nowhere's safe any more. All that's going to happen is that we'll be chased from place to place until one of us gets killed. So no, I'm not all right, thanks for asking.'

'Aven—' began Fern.

'Oh, what's the point?' said Aven. 'Why don't we just give up?'

Nobody could reply. Everything Aven said was true.

Sylvan sank down on his haunches and gazed moodily out of the door into the grey morning. Maybe they should give up, he thought. Maybe they were struggling for nothing. Wouldn't it be easier to just let go? He looked around at the dejected faces of his brother and sisters and saw their tiredness. River sounds filled the silence in their little space. Sylvan listened intently, but the Great River's song remained bland, formless, and dissonant, as if she were reflecting their mood back at them. There was something about that dissonance, though, he thought. It sounded as if something was subtly but firmly out of balance. Was she trying to tell him something? He frowned, and as he listened he found his gaze resting on Fodur: Fodur who had risked his life for them to find out information about the Singers' colonies and who had risked his life further to save Orris. They owed the rat a lot, he realized. And here he was barely breathing, lying under a scant cover of leaves while they did nothing. That wasn't fair and it wasn't right. They owed Fodur more than that. The instant the thought crossed his mind, the dissonance rang loudly and faded to nothing. Sinethis was gone. But Sylvan had the unmistakable feeling that she had given him a message. He thought he understood.

'What do rats eat?' he said.

'What's that got to do with anything,' demanded Aven. 'Didn't you hear what I said?'

'Yes, I did hear,' said Sylvan, 'and I want the same things that you do. And if it was up to me I might be tempted to give up. But I can't. And we can't.'

'What are you talking about?'

'We can't give up on Fodur. If it weren't for him, Orris would probably be dead. We owe him. So we're going to look after him until he's well again.'

'Why? So that he can be snaffled by a mink the second he recovers?'

'No. The point is that it's not our choice whether he lives or dies. It's his choice. It's our fault he's like this so it's up to us to get him well again. We owe him. And if you won't help him then I will. Orris?'

'Yes, Sylvan.'

'He's going to need to drink. Can you find some way to

get water in here?' Orris nodded. 'Good. Fern, what have we seen him eating?'

Fern blinked. 'Erm . . . as far as I can tell he eats almost anything. But he seemed to like worms and beetles.'

'Right. Can you see if you can catch something for him?' She nodded. 'Aven, we still need your help. Not for us, but for Fodur.'

'Doing what?'

'Finding him some more cover. Making him warm.'

Aven said nothing.

'Please? Look, after he's better you can despair all you want. But he needs us. And if our positions were reversed he wouldn't give up on us, would he?'

Aven glared at Sylvan. Then a wry smile spread across her face. 'Sometimes,' she said, 'you talk utter weasel-poo. You have no idea whether he'd give up on us or not, do you?'

'No,' Sylvan admitted. 'But I thought it might persuade you to help.'

Aven sighed. 'All right. I'll see what I can do.'

'Great. See if you can get him warm.' He faced all of them. 'OK, we'll go out for as little time as we can. If you're hungry there's a patch of reeds not far down the bank. Otherwise I'll see you back here as soon as possible. OK?'

The others nodded.

'Good. Let's see if we can get our rat back on his feet, shall we?'

THE JOURNEY

Sylvan surveyed their hollow tree. Fodur's condition was largely unchanged. He was barely breathing and had not woken up at any stage, but now he was lying under a thick cover of dry moss and leaves. The wound had stopped bleeding and was beginning to clot, and Aven had cleaned the rest of the blood from Fodur's fur. Orris had, with great care, carried water back from the Great River in his mouth and laid it in the hollow of a leaf in front of Fodur's nose. Fern had managed to find some beetle grubs and worms and carried them into the tree. She spat them out with distaste and went to fetch more. Sylvan had trouble getting the things to keep still and ended up rolling a stone onto them to stop them from escaping. The rest of the time, while the others were out, he spent excavating earth beneath the tree, tunnelling down into the musty soil. It felt surprisingly good, using his teeth to gnaw down into it, shoving the soil aside and behind him with his paws. He aimed the tunnel so that it would come back up the other side of the tree. If they were going to be hiding there for any time, he wanted to have a way out.

Finally they were all gathered back in the small space. They looked tired but happier than before. Even Aven kept checking Fodur, making sure he was not too hot or cold. Fodur, however, had still not woken.

The voles looked from one to the other. None of them were quite sure what to do next.

'I think we should wake him,' said Fern. 'He needs to drink.'

'I'll do it,' said Orris. He had taken Fodur's injury as his own personal responsibility. Sylvan could see that he wouldn't be happy until the rat was well again. If he ever was. Orris walked to Fodur's shoulder and gently shook him. The rat did not respond. He shook him again and called his name. Fodur's ears flicked and one of his eyes cracked open. It roved around, before finally focusing on Orris's worried face. A muscle twitched in the rat's cheek, a ghost of a smile. Then he coughed and a croaking sound escaped his lips, as if he were trying to speak. Then he closed his eyes again.

'Orris,' said Sylvan, quietly, nodding at the water.

'Oh yes,' said Orris. 'Sorry.' He went to fetch the leaf, dragging it with extreme care until Fodur's muzzle was almost resting on it. 'Water,' he said.

Fodur opened his mouth and his pink tongue lapped at the water. He drank weakly at first, then with thirsty gulps. Orris pulled the leaf a fraction further forwards so that the remaining drops were within reach. When Fodur had drained the leaf he let out a breath like a sigh and closed his eyes.

'Are you hungry, Fodur?' asked Aven, tentatively.

'N-n.'

'Well, we'll get you more water. And there'll be food for when you're a bit better,' she said.

Fodur gave an almost imperceptible nod. A few moments later he had fallen asleep once more.

Sylvan cleared his throat. 'I think we should get him some more water and then we've done as much as we can for a while. We'll get some sleep. I'll keep the first watch.'

The next morning Fodur woke up for just long enough to drink some more water and fall back to sleep. Sylvan went back to his tunnel and the others spent the day fetching more water and feeding, but staying close to the tree, waiting for any sign from their injured friend.

In the early evening, Fodur raised his head.

'I's hungry,' he announced. His ears were flat to his skull and his fur was matted. He didn't look exactly happy, thought Sylvan, but there was a brightness in his eyes and somehow he looked a bit like a rat on the mend. Aven ran to the rock where they had stored the grubs and Orris selected one for Fodur, who pushed himself up on his forefeet, weaving unsteadily. He gobbled the grub up and took another drink of water.

'Is another, please?'

He ate the second, and then a third and fourth, before drinking again. Then he lowered his head onto his forepaws.

'Thanks you,' he said, and fell asleep.

Fodur awoke just before dawn the next morning. The voles had only just risen when he opened his eyes and he pulled himself stiffly into a sitting position. They watched him with a growing sense of excitement.

'How are you feeling?' asked Fern.

The rat managed a wan smile. 'Has been better. Leg hurts.'

'It's nice to see you awake,' said Aven.

'Yes,' agreed Sylvan, 'it really is.'

Orris said nothing. He stared at Fodur and shifted from paw to paw, uncertainly. Fodur slowly swivelled his head until he was looking at Orris.

'Tells you, I did. Speaking with rats not so good for Fodur.'

Orris ducked his head. 'I'm sorry,' he mumbled. A tear leaked out of the corner of his eye and crept down his muzzle. 'I shouldn't have asked. And I should have been braver. I put you in danger and didn't help enough. I'm so sorry.'

'I knows it,' said Fodur, quietly. 'But Fodur remembers. You takes Fodur from river, gets him safe. And Singers feed him and drink him. Fodur knows it. They does this for rat and rat is grateful. You is rat friends. So thinks you should not be sorry. Is nothing be owing between friends.'

Fodur smiled at Orris, and Sylvan could see he meant it. Orris took a tentative step forwards and he and Fodur touched noses. Then Orris backed away, amazed and happy.

'Fodur has good things for Singers,' said Fodur. 'I knows things. I speaks with ratlings. Sometimes know-nothings know something.'

'Is this about Sinnerzurrunslun?' asked Orris, excitedly.

Fodur gave him a flat look. Then he nodded. 'Is,' he confirmed. 'Ratlings says that they has Singers upriver. They says also they has Singers in fields.' Fodur gestured with his chin, out of the tree and away from the Great River. 'Is Singers thataway, they says.'

'In the fields?' said Aven. 'But that's impossible!'

Fodur shook his head. 'I not speak with them long, but they says of a place where river splits and leads to land of water and Singers. Is rat tale, and rat tales is tricksy. But mayhaps this wetted land exist. Mayhaps is new home.'

Sylvan gazed at Fodur. Could there really be another colony of Singers nearby? And a colony in fields, away from the Great River? He couldn't picture what that would be like, but the idea filled him with hope. Fodur closed his eyes again, exhausted. Sylvan turned to the others, eyes shining.

'Sounds good.'

'Oh, come on,' said Aven. 'They were rats, Sylvan. You heard him: "the river splits". I have never heard of anything like that. They were probably wrong, or even if they weren't, the mink could have got there first. We know there are Singers on the Great River, but in fields? It sounds weird. I say we keep going downflow.'

'I don't know,' said Fern, thoughtfully. 'It might be worth looking. We don't know if the place exists but we do know that there is a mink on the Great River. If we carry on downflow, it could just show up again. If we can find this wetted land we might be in with a chance.'

'I still reckon it's a risk.'

'If you hadn't noticed, everything we're doing is a risk,' said Sylvan. 'We have no idea what's round the next corner. All I'm saying is Fodur's given us somewhere to aim for, and it's close. I think we should try to at least look for it.'

Even in the moments since Fodur had told them of the

new colony, the feeling had been growing in him that that was where they had to go: not downstream or upstream, but into the unknown, away from the Great River altogether. He could feel the familiar urge of Sinethis guiding him. It felt right.

'But what about Fodur?' asked Orris. 'He's not going anywhere in the state he's in. We can't leave him here.'

'Oh. No, of course we can't,' said Sylvan. In his excitement he had almost forgotten.

'So we're stuck here until Fodur gets better?' said Aven.

'Not quite,' said Sylvan, thoughtfully. 'There's no reason one of us can't go out and have a look around while we're waiting for him to recover, is there?'

Aven narrowed her eyes. 'If I was being suspicious, I'd reckon you just want to go off exploring. Why not all go together when he's better?'

'Because five of us, one injured, wandering around the Great River not knowing where we're going isn't a great idea,' said Sylvan.

'That's what we've been doing,' said Aven. 'It seemed fine until you thought you could have an adventure without us.'

'Look,' said Sylvan, trying not to lose his temper, 'this isn't about me wanting an adventure. This is about us surviving. One vole travelling fast can have a look around and come back with more information. Then we'll know where to go.'

'I don't like it,' said Fern. 'But I think Sylvan's right. If you go, though, I'm coming too.'

'What?' said Sylvan.

'I said I'm coming with you. Two of us will be safer than one. And if something happens to one of us then the other one can come back for the others. It's not that I want to. I'm scared just thinking about it, but someone needs to go with you.' She smiled, tightly. 'After all, you'll need somebody there to do the thinking.'

Sylvan was speechless for a moment. Then he nodded. 'Fine. We'll go together then. All agreed?' The others nodded, reluctantly. 'Good. Fern, I suppose we should make a start soon.'

The decision made, they went out to feed. Sylvan didn't know when they would have the chance again, so they stocked up while they could. The feeding patch was just about sufficient: a few sparse reeds, some iris, and a little watercress. Even with Sylvan and Fern gone, the remaining food would only last a few days.

He turned to Aven and Orris. 'We'll be back. It might be a day or two, but we'll be back. And hopefully we'll have good news.'

Aven tried to look unconcerned. Orris nodded, stiffly. They touched noses and made their goodbyes. Then Sylvan and Fern

turned and set off downflow. As they went, Sylvan took a last look back at his brother and sister, still standing on the bank. He felt a wrench at leaving them behind. *It's OK*, he told himself. *It'll all be fine*. But still a sense of unease filled him. He would be a lot happier when they were all back together.

Sylvan and Fern travelled all morning along the Great River, covering the ground as quickly as they could. Perhaps they were lulled by the breeze, or the tree-dappled sunlight. Or perhaps they would never have spotted it anyway. Whatever the reason, they barely had time to scramble for cover. Hunched down in the reeds, Sylvan glanced at Fern. Her expression mirrored his own: a mixture of fear and exhilaration.

The animal was huge, and moved with terrible grace, rolling languidly in the water and diving deep. After each dive it returned to the surface with a crayfish in its jaws. It carried them to the bank, turned them with clever paws and crunched through their shells and into their flesh. A large pile of empty crayfish remains lay at the water's edge, claws and carapaces stacked in a heap.

'What is it?' hissed Sylvan when it had dived for another.

'Otter,' said Fern, her voice full of wonder.

It could only be an otter. Amongst the Folk, otters were a myth that mothers used in stories to send pleasant thrills of fear through their wide-eyed pups: a powerful enemy, but one which took River Singers only rarely, preferring to feast on the giant fish which they hunted in pools. Sylvan had never expected to actually see one.

'It's amazing,' he said.

The otter's glossy fur, stiff whiskers, and gigantic, nimble frame made Sylvan feel almost ridiculously small and insignificant. Everything about it exuded power and poise. If it knew that two young Singers were so close it could snap out their lives in an instant, but Sylvan found he was not really afraid. With so many crayfish it wouldn't bother with two small voles. And while the otter was there, they were probably safe also from the other enemies. Nothing would dare to tangle with something like that.

For a long while the only sounds were the crunch of crayfish, the breeze in the trees, and the burbling of the Great River, but eventually the otter discarded its last empty shell and ran its claws over its whiskers to clean them. It stood for a moment, surveying its territory, and then bounded off and away, threading downflow through the undergrowth. Sylvan and Fern exchanged delighted looks. An otter! They must be two of the few Singers ever to see one.

Cautiously, they made their way out of their cover. Fern headed past the pile of crayfish and over to a tree branch where the otter had been sitting. It had deposited a reddish dropping there, coated in a sharp, musky-sweet smell. Fern sniffed at it. Sylvan, eager to be moving now the danger had passed, watched her with growing exasperation. Why was she so obsessed with sniffing things?

Fern caught his expression. 'You think I'm wasting my time, don't you?'

'I didn't say anything,' he protested. 'But OK, I don't really see the point.'

'The point,' said Fern, 'is that we nearly ran straight into an otter. We didn't see or hear it. Next time the smell might warn us.'

'Fine. Now can we go, please?'

'Of course.' Fern pushed past him and set off. Sylvan followed. They put more distance between themselves and the hollow tree. Sylvan felt a strange mixture of emotions.

He was certain they were doing the right thing; the quiet downflow pull of the Great River told him that. But he was worried. Orris, Aven, and Fodur were increasingly far behind them and he and Fern were heading who-knew-where to find a new home. He felt as though he had left a part of himself back with the others. If anything happened to them while they were gone, he would never forgive himself.

Fern fell in alongside him. As if she had been reading his thoughts she said, 'You know, I used to think that you were just a careless male.' She stepped around a tree root. 'But you're doing really well. I thought I should say so.'

Sylvan wasn't quite sure what to make of the compliment. 'Oh. Thanks. You're doing all right too.'

They walked for a bit in silence.

'But I still think you spend too much time with your nose in other people's droppings.'

Fern made a disgusted noise and pulled ahead of him. But Sylvan thought that he caught a smile on her face.

After that they spoke little, moving quickly, pausing to feed when they could. As the afternoon passed, the trees closed ranks overhead, and the grasses became sparser. The voles became more subdued. They were seeking a split in the Great River, leading to a wetted land. In the gloom beneath the branches, such a place felt a long way off. Towards the evening, clouds built up. The breeze stiffened to a strong wind, making the trees toss their branches and the bushes shake. Stray gusts ruffled their whiskers and the fur on their backs. The constant sussurration masked the other sounds, which mingled and dissolved, becoming muted and indistinct. Sylvan cast an apprehensive look around him. This was not good. If something were to find them now, they might not hear it until it was too late. The Great River, too, was changed. Her banks were now steep and earthen, almost bare of foliage. Her waters were white and rapid, rushing in disarray, tumbling over themselves and swirling around rocks and trees. An unhappy knot formed in Sylvan's belly. Sinethis did not look as if she would welcome a diving Singer here.

Sylvan picked up the pace and Fern followed, both hoping that each bend would bring brighter prospects. But none came. Soon enough the light began to fail, and the River Singers faced a stark choice. They stopped at the first shelter they could find. It was a clump of brambles, near the top of the bank, well away from the water's edge.

'Well,' said Sylvan, raising his voice above the wind. 'It's cover.'

For a second it looked as though Fern would argue, but instead she nodded.

'No choice,' she said. 'Shame.'

Seeing the expression on her face, unhappy but determined, Sylvan felt a rush of affection for his sister.

He nudged her with a paw and smiled.

'Don't worry,' he said. 'It'll be OK. It's only for one night.'

Fern returned a wan smile. 'Come on then.'

Together they made their way up the bank and surveyed their quarters. The brambles formed a wide, overhanging lip, leaving a roomy gap between their base and the ground. Sylvan wished that they reached lower. They wouldn't offer much protection, but it was the best they had. Together they excavated a small hollow inside and found some dried grass which they tugged under the brambles. The grasses would keep them warm, and under the brambles the sound of the wind was not so loud. But it was far from what either of them would have chosen.

Fern put a brave face on it. 'Better than nothing.'

'Yeah. Just about. Let's see if we can get comfortable.'

They settled for the night, nestling together for warmth. But still an unhappy feeling grew in Sylvan which he could not dislodge. This was a place where something could go very wrong. And so, tired and aching, he stared out into the outside world, watching as the fading daylight leached the colour from the world.

He saw the fox before he heard it. It ghosted out of the twilight, picking its way delicately along the water's edge
below them, one foot before the next, nose to the ground. As
it approached its features sharpened into horrible reality:
an immense creature with a long muzzle and ears pricked
forwards. Sylvan went cold. The fox paused for a moment at
a spot where they had stopped earlier. It scented all around
and raised its head, listening. Then it trotted onwards, following their trail. Sylvan glanced at Fern. She was awake and
he saw that she too had understood. If it followed their scent
it could find them. And they could do nothing but watch. If
they went out into the open it would surely take them. The
fox stepped around a bush, over a fallen branch and trotted
along the edge of the bank below their hiding place.

It moved past them and on. Sylvan almost shook with
relief. In a burrow a fox could not hope to take a Singer,
but here in the open, this far from the Great River . . . He
shuddered. He turned to Fern to say something, but she
tensed, grabbing for him.

'It's coming back.'

To his horror, Sylvan saw that she was right. The fox had only briefly lost their trail. Now it had turned towards them.

'It's going to find us,' said Fern, trembling. She cast a despairing look at Sylvan. 'What do we do?'

Sylvan fought down the rising panic. It was seeking them in their hiding place. Once it found the trail, it would be led straight to them.

'We have to wait,' he hissed. 'It won't fit under the brambles.'

They watched the fox pace backwards and forwards across the river bank.

'They won't stop it,' said Fern. 'We have to get to the Great River.'

'Here? She'll kill us. Did you see how fast her flow is?'

'Better her than the fox.'

Sylvan nodded. It was the only way. The fox could never catch them in the water. But between them and the water was an incline and then an expanse of flat, open ground. They would have to run for it. And then the rapids. The options were stark.

The fox stopped pacing and raised its head, staring straight at them. It lowered its nose and sniffed at the plants further up the bank. Its tail went up and it scented again, excitedly. Then it started to climb the bank. Sylvan tensed.

'Ready?'

The fox drew closer. Fern nodded and crouched down, ready to sprint for the water.

Closer.

'If anything happens to me, get back to the others,' Sylvan hissed.

Closer.

'No. We're too far. We need to find the other Singers.'

'What?'

Closer.

'Just do it! Promise me.'

'All right, I—'

The fox leapt, thrusting its muzzle beneath the brambles and deep into their nest. Fern leapt aside as its jaws snapped, missing her and closing instead on a spiky stem. It gave a terrible yelp and withdrew. From between the stems, Sylvan could see the beast pawing at its mouth. Then the fox moved to where the brambles were thinnest. It began to dig. Earth flew out from beneath it. The hole in front of them grew at a frightening speed. Sylvan ran desperately around their space, seeking any escape. But the brambles were bound tightly on three sides. The only exit was past the fox. They backed away as far as they could. The fox clawed at the earth, then thrust its muzzle in again, snapping at the voles, who jumped away, twisting and squeaking, hurling themselves aside to evade its teeth. It withdrew and began digging once more.

Sylvan panted with terror. 'Next time. Next time we run.'

They crouched low waiting in dread for their chance. Outside the fox tore at the ground, digging for its meal. The paws stopped.

'Now!' screamed Sylvan and dashed headlong for the right-hand side of the entrance. He burst into the twilight, pelting down the slope, hurling himself towards the water. From the corner of his eye he saw Fern to his left sprinting hard but dropping behind. And behind them the fox, wrong-footed, whirled about and leapt in pursuit of the fleeing voles. The world flew at Sylvan, plants, rocks, soil, all of it rushing at him in a chaos of terror. He gave everything he had, dashing for the water. The fox panted behind him. The water was a line in his vision, a glistening expanse, and then he was in the air, diving towards the surface. In that instant, somewhere almost lost behind him, he heard a tiny snapping noise, like the crack of a reed stem. And then he burst through the surface and plunged down through the depths, pulling at the Great River with frantic strokes.

In this place, Sinethis raged. She fell upon him with a snarl, hurling him aside, beating him down, twisting him and tossing him aside. Sylvan kicked out, flailing at her, battling

for his life. She flung him away, and for an instant he broke the surface, gasped at air, before she plucked him down into the dark. He smashed against a rock and was dragged into an undertow, rolling along the river bed. He kicked again, his feet gaining purchase on something, and was thrust back to the surface. He drew a shuddering lungful before she crashed over his head, pulling him down into her depths.

How long he fought with Sinethis, and how far she carried him, he could not tell. Time and again he clawed to the surface for a scant, rasping breath and time and again she dragged him back. And now he was growing weaker. His legs paddled feebly. His lungs burned with the need to breathe. Panic began to take hold. He could no longer sense which way was up, where the air lay. The world slipped aside, and a strange blackness welled up until there was nothing but the darkness and the deluge of Sinethis's song. She sang in him, louder than she had ever been, her melodies twining deeply through his heart. She sang a song of savagery and peace, of raging torrents and burbling trickles, cataracts and calm. She sang of life, a strident tune, its notes strong, bright, and gleaming. She sang of death, the notes muted, dissolving and mingling with the others, lost in the eternal whole. Even as she poured into Sylvan, his note still struggled to be heard. But it was fading.

You are a child of the Great River. You sing a song as brief as day. You are a River Singer and you are mine. Join me. Become my melody. We have flowed together, but there is further now to go. Flow with me to the end. I will carry you there. This too is my way.

Her voice was soothing. She curled around him and cradled him like a child. In the peaceful cadence of her music she urged him to stop, to give in, to let go. The simplest thing in the world would be to be drawn into her. They would drift onward, together as they had always been. But even as Sylvan drifted, an image came to him of Orris and Aven, huddling in a tree, waiting for his return. He had said that he would look after them, and he remembered Sinethis's bargain. She had said that she would make him strong, told him to follow her. So he had flowed with her. He had given her his sacrifice every step of the way. And this was how she rewarded him? What of Aven and Orris? What of Fern? Almost lost in the myriad threads, Sylvan's solitary note began to tremble with anger.

It wasn't enough, was it? Everything I've done wasn't enough. We live as sacrifice and if we don't give our lives you take them. Is that it? I have been strong. I followed you faithfully. And this is what I get? I kept my bargain, I was as strong as I could be. And you cheated me.

No response. Sylvan was incensed. *Do you think you've got what you want?* he shouted. *Well, you haven't. You took my strength from me but you won't take me. I'm mine, not yours. My life is not your sacrifice, it's theirs. I live for them. We had a bargain, and you betrayed me. So now I'm mine, not yours. Let me loose or take me, but I will never be yours.*

Sinethis's response rang through him. Sylvan heard a ripple of amusement in her voice. *Very well, then, River Singer. A bargain it was and a bargain it remains. But you are mine and always will be. You live for whom you choose, but your sacrifice shall always be mine. If you wish it, though, your sacrifice may continue. For a time. Is this what you choose?*

It is, he said.

Then the bargain is made. You wished to be strong and I have made you strong. Continue, then, and follow where I lead. Live well, River Singer.

Sylvan was caught up and swirled towards the surface in an agony of spasming muscles. He smashed his way into the air and gasped down lungful after wonderful lungful.

Around him the Great River eased to a swift, smooth flow and Sylvan was shunted aside into a quiet backwater. He opened his eyes and his heart gave a thump of joy. He was within reach of a ragged fringe of reeds. With his final reserves he hauled his bedraggled body onto the shore, crawled into the blissful shelter, and keeled onto his side, gasping. For a long while he lay there, huddled tight and shivering, his mind and body numb.

The moon rose, casting a silver light which shimmered on the water, even as the darkness pooled around Sylvan's prone body. Eventually, Sylvan's senses returned enough that he could push himself upright. His muscles ached. He shivered. He surveyed his position. He was in a sparse stand of reeds in the calm back-eddy where Sinethis had released him. To his right, the Great River rushed downflow, her current swift, but with none of the turbulence that had so nearly taken his life. He looked to his left. He blinked. The moon illuminated a sight he had never before seen. His first thought was that

the Great River had split, that she had made another channel
which led away across the fields. But as he stared, wide-eyed,
he saw that this was a separate stream which flowed into
Sinethis, mingling its waters with hers.

Sylvan sat back on his haunches, trying to comprehend
what he was seeing. Another river. Could it be that Sinethis
was only one among many? Or perhaps all the waters were

part of her. Even as these thoughts ran through him, his
certainty grew that he had been brought here for a reason.
Here a new river ran into Sinethis from across the fields. And
Fodur had spoken of a place where the Great River splits,
leading to a wetted land. Here, at last, he might find the other
River Singers. A small spark of excitement began to form in
him. But even as it did, a cruel wind whipped through the
reeds, chilling his wet fur. He was alive, it reminded him, but
he was alone, and far from safe.

Alone, he thought. *Fern. Where is Fern?*
In his battle with Sinethis he had had
no time to consider her. They had been
running together, he to one side and she
to the other. Sylvan had dived. She had been
right behind him. Surely she had made it to the
water? He peered into the night, as if to catch sight
of her. But then he remembered the snapping sound,
so like a dried reed stem. The memory made him
go cold. He had never before heard a sound like
that. It had sounded final, as if something had been
broken beyond repair. Fern might not have
escaped the fox. That snapping noise . . . No, he
must not think it. But even if she had escaped,
even if she had made it to the water, Sinethis could
have drowned her. And if not then she might arrive
here, or she might be anywhere upflow or have
been carried further down.

He wanted desperately to go back
and look for her. But if he did and the
fox was there, he would be
in terrible danger. Or he
could miss her in the night.
What if he left and Fern

arrived after him? What if he never found her? And what of his promise to her, that he would seek the other River Singers? Sylvan stood in an agony of indecision, torn between despair, hope, and his responsibility to Fern and the others. He hesitated, hoping for a sign, anything, that might tell him of Fern's fate. No sign came. He saw nothing. And no sound came to him in the night but the wind in the trees and Sinethis's eternal song.

What can I do? he thought. And as if in answer, the memory of Sinethis's final words returned to him. *Follow where I lead*, she had said. And with the memory came his decision. Sinethis had brought him to this place. She had done so for a reason. And Fern had made him promise to find the other Singers. He had to see it through. And there was still hope. Perhaps she had survived and would find him. Or perhaps she would return to the hollow tree and wait for him. Perhaps. But the decision was made. He had to go on without her.

Sylvan stood. He turned his back to the Great River. He pointed his nose up the new channel. Then, not caring for danger or the darkness, he began to push his way through the plants. He headed upflow, following this new stream that cut through the fields, away from Sinethis, her coldness and his memories. He was alone, holding his promise in his heart. He would find the other Singers. He would return to his family. He would make them all safe.

PART 3
THE WETTED LAND

Mistress Marjoram's morning had been rather irritating, what with one thing and another. As a result she was in a terrible mood when that vagabond male arrived in her territory. Later on Camilla had been quite upset but, thought Mistress Marjoram, had only herself to blame. Certainly it wasn't her own fault; of that she was quite sure. After all, she had struggled all her life in this difficult territory. She had inherited most of it from her mother, whom she couldn't help wishing had been more proactive in acquiring somewhere with decent burrows or a more upflow location. Oh, it was all right, she supposed. The territory was at least on the river, far better than the marsh, and there were some good eating places. Also, its position meant that she didn't often have to fight off other females. She could do, perhaps, with a few more male visitors from time to time, and she would have liked the food plants downflow to be taller. Her main objection was that she really did not like living so close to all those horrible trees. Who knew what could come out of them? Yes, she thought, hers was a trying position, made especially so by Camilla, her daughter. That girl was a constant worry. No matter how strict she was with her, Camilla never seemed to pull herself together. Too soft-hearted by half.

'It's about time,' Mistress Marjoram told her daughter, 'that you were out finding yourself a territory. You can't expect to stay around here all your life.'

'No, Mother.'

'When I was your age I already had a territory of my own.'

'Yes, Mother. But that's only because—'

Mistress Marjoram cut her daughter short. 'Don't "Yes, Mother" me, Camilla. There are plenty of spaces on the river for a bright young vole like you. You're just going to have to go and find one for yourself. That's all there is to it.'

'Yes, Mother.' Then Camilla gave a small sigh and wandered off, leaving Mistress Marjoram shaking her head. Young these days. No backbone. Mistress Marjoram put Camilla from her mind. There were duties to be observed and it was high time somebody checked on the downflow edge of the territory. Not that there was much point. No Singer in her right mind would go close to the trees but that did not mean she should let standards slip. Mistress Marjoram bustled away from the home burrow, huffing her way down to the edge of her world. As she drew into the shade she felt the familiar sting of trepidation. She did not know—naturally—what lay beyond, but she did know that it could not come to any good.

Crunch.

Mistress Marjoram stopped dead in shock. The noise was unmistakable. One of the Folk was feeding. And in *her* iris patch. The cheek of it! She puffed herself up to her full, impressive size. She had no idea how the Singer had come so far down into her territory but she did know that it was going to regret trespassing. She pushed forwards, bullying her way through the plants, not caring how much noise she made. By the time she shouldered into the iris patch, the Singer had heard her and was waiting. She drew to a halt and surveyed the bedraggled excuse for a water vole that faced her. The bedraggled excuse in question blinked stupidly, as if in a daze or unable to believe its eyes.

'You're a Singer,' said the male, slowly.

'Of course I'm a River Singer,' snapped Mistress Marjoram. 'And so are you, as far as I can tell. What are you doing in my territory?'

The male seemed not to register what she had said.

'You're a Singer. You live here?'

Mistress Marjoram rolled her eyes. The male was clearly an idiot.

'Yes, that's right. As I said: this is my territory, and you are feeding in it. And, if you haven't noticed, you don't have my permission. Would you mind telling me what you think you're doing?'

The male belatedly put down the piece of iris he was holding.

'I'm sorry. I walked all night and I was hungry.'

His face was a strange mixture of expressions: amazement, sadness, fatigue. He swayed on the spot a little. Mistress Marjoram wondered if he was quite well. Still, whatever his state he needn't think he was getting away with anything.

'Didn't you see the boundary marker?' she demanded. 'Don't you have a place of your own to feed in?'

'No. Not really. If I had, I would have done things differently. Sorry.'

Mistress Marjoram considered him. He was almost adult, with a big frame, but terribly thin and unkempt. He looked like a ruffian. But then his appearance was offset by the quietly polite way in which he spoke. He was certainly one of the oddest voles she had ever met.

'Where did you come from? I've never seen you before. You're not one of those horrible youngsters from the marsh, are you?'

He did not quite seem the type, though, she thought. That could only be a good thing. She considered any Singer who lived in that sprawling network of ditches as irredeemably vulgar. If any of the marsh males came sniffing around her territory she would send them packing. They simply did not have the good breeding of the proper River Singers.

'I've never been to a marsh. Is that the Wetted Land? The place with grass and water?'

'Are you attempting to be humorous with me?' she asked, archly.

'What? Oh. No, I'm really not. But please could you answer my question?'

Mistress Marjoram sighed. 'Yes, the marsh is the place with water and the grass. It also has ditches and tussock sedges, if that helps?'

Her attempt at sarcasm apparently did not register.

'Does it?' he said. 'That sounds good. We don't have ditches and tussocks where I come from.'

He gazed hungrily down at the iris, as if wondering whether it would be rude to start eating again. *Maybe he really is an idiot*, thought Mistress Marjoram. Yes. Now she thought of it that was clearly the explanation. He was an idiot—it accounted for all his behaviour. But what had he meant by "where I come from"?

'And where are you from, exactly?'

The male gestured behind him to the woodland. 'There,' he said. 'We—I used to live on the Great River.'

Ah. There, you see? It was just as she suspected.

'I don't think you did, did you?' she said as kindly as she could manage. 'You see, this is the Great River right here, isn't it. You're standing next to her. So we all live on the Great River, really, don't we?'

The male stared at her for so long that she thought he had gone into a stupor.

'This isn't the Great River,' he said. 'It's too small.'

Mistress Marjoram was outraged. The idiot was contradicting her when she was clearly right. She gazed across to the other bank, which was fully the length of three Singers away. Assured of her correctness, she was about to turn back to argue when an ungainly crashing sound behind her announced that Camilla was approaching. That, thought Mistress Marjoram, was all she needed.

'What's going on, Mother? I heard . . . Oh, sorry. I didn't realize we had a guest.'

Mistress Marjoram rolled her eyes. Guest, indeed. She sometimes wondered if this girl was ever going to be fit for a territory. She dropped her voice to a hiss. 'He's not a guest, he's an idiot. And he's eating our plants. We must get rid of him.'

'He looks half-starved, Mother,' Camilla whispered. 'We can't possibly turn him away in that state.' Then, to Mistress Marjoram's horror, Camilla raised her voice and called, 'Hello. Who are you?'

The male, who had grabbed for some food the second Mistress Marjoram's back was turned, quickly dropped it again. He chewed and swallowed before saying, 'My name is Sylvan.'

'I'm Camilla,' said Camilla.

'I'm pleased to meet you. You have no idea how much. But I'm very hungry. Would it be all right if I ate some iris?'

'Of course,' said Camilla. 'Anything you like.'

'This is still my territory,' said Mistress Marjoram softly.

'The poor thing's hungry. We should let him have some food.'

'But that's my iris.'

'There's enough iris to go round, Mother. We wouldn't want to be inhospitable, would we?'

Mistress Marjoram drew herself up. She had no idea what had got into her daughter, but she was quite sure that she had had enough of youngsters today. 'Well,' she said, as haughtily as she could manage, 'I'm quite sure that *you* wouldn't, at any rate. Personally, I have better things to do than to watch some vagabond stranger eating all my best food.'

She stalked off, leaving Camilla and that strange Sylvan male to it. If she was so taken with him she could look after him. From behind her came the clear and insufferable sounds of a starving River Singer feeding ravenously in a stand of her prime iris. That she had never fed there herself was entirely beside the point. It was the principle of the thing. She ignored the noises and shouldered her way up to the far end of her territory. At least up there she was only likely to meet Singers of good breeding.

It was evening before Mistress Marjoram encountered Camilla again. In the intervening time she had quite forgotten about the unfortunate episode of the morning. But seeing the distracted expression on her daughter's face it all came horribly back.

'So. Have you finally finished being "hospitable"?'

'Oh, hello, Mother. Yes, thank you. Sylvan had to go, though.'

'Just as well. Between you and me I suspect he was a little bit simple.'

'He was just lost, Mother, that's all. He wanted to know all about the marsh and things, and how many Singers there are there. It sounded like he'd never heard of the place. He also asked about something called a mink but I said we didn't have any. I hope that was all right.'

'Humph. Anyway, the important thing is that he's gone, has he?'

'Yes, Mother. I invited him to stay but he said he just needed some sleep and then he had to go back and find the rest of his family.'

'Well, at least he had that amount of propriety, unlike certain young voles I could mention who go around offering perfect strangers nests in their mother's territory. I mean really, what were you thinking, Camilla?'

Camilla's expression grew a little firmer. 'I was thinking that if I was in his position I'd want someone to offer me some food.'

But Mistress Marjoram was not listening. Her brow furrowed.

'Camilla?' she said. 'Are you sure he's gone? He certainly didn't come this way.'

Camilla sighed. 'He went the other way.'

'Don't sigh, Camilla. And what do you mean other way? What other way?'

'Through the woods.'

Well, thought Mistress Marjoram, that settled it. She knew she hadn't liked the look of that young vole. Through the woods? No River Singer worth speaking to would go anywhere near those woods. She drew a satisfied breath and fixed her daughter with what she hoped was a penetrating stare.

'Well, then. I dare say that if young Mr Sylvan has headed into those woods we won't be seeing him again. They're completely impenetrable. Full of all sorts of ghastly things. He's probably already been taken.' Mistress Marjoram squinted up at the setting sun. 'In any case, it's past time we were heading back to the burrow.'

Camilla did not respond. Mistress Marjoram wondered briefly if she might be upset about something. Probably. She usually was. But she couldn't expect her mother to put up with a constant stream of vagabonds just to keep her happy. Mistress Marjoram set off for the burrow, and after a moment her daughter followed.

'It's like I keep telling you,' said Mistress Marjoram. 'You need to go out and find yourself a territory. Then you'll be able to give food to any male you like.'

'Yes, Mother,' said Camilla, dutifully.

Mistress Marjoram thought for a second. 'But not any from the marsh.'

'Oh, Mother.'

He had found River Singers. He had found them. The thought kept repeating over and over in Sylvan's mind. He had done it. Everything in him was now driving him back up the Great River, upflow to where he had left his family. He had to get back to them. He had to tell them. He forced his tired legs onwards, keeping an eye out for Fern. Every bend of the Great River brought fresh hope that he would find her waiting for him, or else some sign that she had escaped the fox. As he went he scoured the ground for anything, a footprint, a dropping, a piece of feeding sign: anything that would tell him if she was all right. Soon enough, though, he found himself gazing up at the small bramble patch they had sheltered in. Scattered earth still fanned out from the freshly excavated hollow in front of it. He searched the ground, seeking answers among the confusion of fox prints and vole tracks, but he found nothing of use. Fern's tracks ended close to the water's edge. And so did the fox's. No fresh Singer tracks led along the bank, neither up or downflow. He pattered a little way further upflow, to where the waters were calmer, and swam across, hoping for evidence that Fern had escaped to the other side. But there was nothing. Eventually he had no choice but

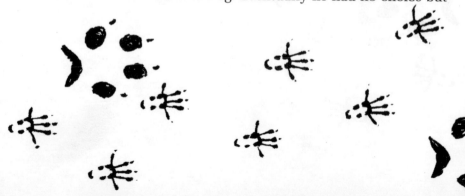

to give in, and continue on his way. He walked mechanically, his legs shoving at the earth, carrying him onwards. There was still hope, around every bend. Perhaps when he got back to the others he would find Fern with them, waiting for him. He held the thought like a lifeline. He followed it, step by step, back to his family, time blurring in a haze of tiredness. His world narrowed to a solitary goal until he felt nothing but the rhythm of his journey: hiding, scenting, dashing, all of them mere tools to bring him ever closer.

Sylvan was shaken from his daze by a familiar conjunction of bank and river. His legs responded of their own accord, stumbling to a halt even as his head cleared. He knew this place. He had been here only a few days before. Yes. He and Fern had hidden over there. And here was the pile of crayfish remains. They had stood here together  and watched the otter. He could even smell its sweet, musky scent. He was close, now. He was nearly back.

Sylvan was about to continue when something drew his attention. The scene was almost imperceptibly different. It took a few moments to spot it. The pile of discarded crayfish was larger, and the smell was still fresh. A thrill ran through him. He surveyed the clearing. There was no otter to be seen. But it had been here recently. It could still be here. It could be watching. Motionless, Sylvan drew in every last sight, sound, and scent until he was satisfied that there were no enemies nearby. Then, quietly, he slunk down into the tall reeds at the water's edge and began picking his way towards the hollow tree where so many of his hopes rested. He would not make any mistakes. Not now.

So close to his goal, doubts began to creep into Sylvan's mind. What if he got back to the tree and it was empty? What if he arrived and they had all been taken? He tried not to think these thoughts. It was more likely that they'd be there, wasn't it? And that Fern was with them. Yes. She would be there for sure. But the doubts persisted. He was so close, and he had endured so much. All he wanted was to curl up with them, tell them that he had done it, that there were Singers nearby who had never heard of a mink and that soon they would all be safe. He could not believe it, though. Sinethis would never make his life so easy. He glanced over at the Great River. Here she flowed deceptively calmly, but he remembered her other side and his churning, battering ordeal. He turned his head away and concentrated on his path. He spotted a familiar tree branch, fallen into the water. Here too was a small clump where he and Fern had fed, just after leaving. He almost ran up to it. Yes, their feeding sign still lay on the ground, yellowing slightly. Strange, he thought, almost detachedly, that Fern was missing and yet here was something she had made, still lying on the ground. He shoved the thought aside and lifted his head. He was close. Just around the next bend lay the hollowed tree and, Sinethis willing, his family.

He made to set off, but as he did something pulled him up. He listened intently to the sounds of the Great River. Nothing. Everything had gone eerily quiet. The coots and moorhens were silent. No ground birds were calling. As he listened, his ear picked out Sinethis's music. He tried to shut it out but she flowed into him without regard for his wishes. A warning note rang in his mind, a terrible, familiar discord that set every one of his senses alert. It faded in an instant, but it was enough.

Sylvan quivered. Sinethis had spoken, and he had understood. The mink was here. He made for the hollow tree as silently as he could, ready to leap for the water at the first sign of danger. He had no idea what he could do against a mink, but he had to help them, warn them, anything. He crested the final curve and eased through the last stand of reeds to the edge of their cover. He stifled a horrified gasp.

In the bay in front of the tree, stood the mink. It scented the air as if it had every right to be there. It put its nose to the ground and sniffed excitedly around in a circle. It ran towards Sylvan, following a line of vole tracks. Sylvan shrank back. The mink stopped short. It sniffed a few more times and then turned and followed the trail back to the tree, heading for the entrance. Sylvan's muscles clenched. If the mink went in there, and the others were still inside, it would be slaughter. He could not stand by and watch but what could he do, alone against a mink? They would all be killed. What good had Sinethis's warning been? Or perhaps it hadn't even been a warning, just some final cruelty of hers, a last way to torment him.

Is this what you wanted, Sinethis? he cried to her in his mind. *For me to watch them die?*

And Sinethis's angry reply rose up and smashed into him with the force of a winter flood. *No, Singer. I gave you warning. I made you strong. I taught you to fight.*

And Sinethis rushed through him, bearing him up, carrying him from all knowledge of himself. Sylvan screamed a wordless cry into the quiet of the riverbank. He filled it with all of his terror and loss and fury. He filled it with his love for his family. He hurled himself out of the cover and after the mink's retreating form. The mink, at the entrance to the tree, had no time to react before Sylvan flung himself upon it, sinking his teeth deep into the muscles of its leg. Blood and sour musk filled Sylvan's mouth, salty and sickly.

The mink screamed with pain and rage. It whirled and battered Sylvan aside. A momentary weightlessness and then the ground smashed against his ribs. The Great River rang like a bell within him. Then he was up and running, fleeing back the way he had come. The mink lurched in pursuit, limping on its injured leg. Sylvan hurtled through reeds, over roots, under branches, nothing in him now but the need to run, to live. And Sinethis flowed with him, buoying him up and driving him on, as if, once more, he was tumbling in her rapids. If he slowed for an instant she drove at him, urging him faster. Sylvan ran and the mink panted behind him, closing on its prey.

The mink lunged, teeth snapping a fraction behind him. It stumbled and fell on its injured leg, howling with pain.

Sylvan did not glance back but forced himself to greater speed. His breath was ragged and he too stumbled and nearly tripped, barely able to keep his feet. The mink rolled to its feet and leapt back to the chase. It closed on him once more.

Sylvan willed himself faster but his legs refused to obey. The mink's breath was hot on his back. It would have him. He was going to die.

A scent filled Sylvan's nostrils, musky-sweet and strong. He wrenched his head up. His eyes widened. Before him stood the otter. Its giant frame seemed to fill the riverbank. It opened a mouth filled with teeth. It leapt, screaming a challenge. Sylvan barely had time to react. He tried to dodge but his legs, tired beyond endurance, gave way. He fell heavily onto his side and rolled down the bank. He smacked painfully against a tree root and landed with a splash in the Great River. He struggled, gasping and panting, to the surface. He tried to swim across, but the current was too strong. Instead he clawed his way downflow to quieter water and dragged himself out, shivering in terrified exhaustion.

Upflow, shrieks and screams filled the air. For a moment there was silence and then two huge bodies hurtled down the length of the riverbank. The mink crashed into view, pursued by the much larger otter. They thundered past Sylvan's hiding place. For a moment the mink seemed to break free, but the

otter leapt on it and brought it snarling to the ground. They rolled over and over, snapping and clawing, until the mink twisted loose. It rolled to its feet, poised to flee, but the otter smashed into it, driving them both down the bank and into the Great River. Water churned and bodies thrashed. They broke apart for an instant and the otter dived from view. For an instant the mink swam alone in the Great River but then, with a despairing shriek, was plucked below the surface. A trail of bubbles rose, followed by a plume of red, staining the water, frothing and fanning out as it spread.

A limp, dark body bobbed to the surface and was carried downstream, lifeless.

Across the river from Sylvan, the otter pulled itself smoothly onto the bank and shook the water from its fur. It glanced once at the mink's floating corpse, and padded off. Sylvan was alone, filled with amazement. He was alive. He was safe. The mink was dead. He tried to move, but the effort was too great. The world spun about him and everything went very dark and far away. The Great River rang tinnily in his ears and then, as if he had been sucked into murky waters, everything disappeared.

Cold. Noises. Voices. They sounded familiar, but Sylvan couldn't place them. Everything was muzzy and dark. He

began to drift again, but the voices interrupted. They were too loud. He wished they would go away. The words filtered into his mind, uninvited.

'. . . you think he's all right?'

'I don't know. Stop asking stupid questions.'

'Don't take it out on me, it's—'

'Orris!'

'All right, no need to shout.'

'I wasn't shouting, I . . . Look, just lend me a paw, will you?'

A shoving sensation against his flank. His body rolled. He wanted to be left alone. He tried to protest, but he could not quite seem to get the words out. *Leave me alone.*

'Leazmehz,' he said.

'He's alive. Aven, he's alive.'

'I can see he's alive, Orris. I could see that before. But he won't be for much longer unless we can get him inside.'

'Sylvan, wake up, will you?'

'Nzzzz.'

Again, some shoving at Sylvan's flank, this time on both sides. Sylvan's weight was shunted over his feet. He considered trying to stay there but slumped to the ground again. It felt better that way.

'It's no good. He's too heavy.'

'What if I went and got Fodur?'

'Right, Orris. Perfect. What we really need to help us here is a three-legged rat. Brilliant.'

'It's just an idea.'

'Well it was a stupid one. Fodur's only just started walking again. I don't think he's up to carrying a water vole around, is he?'

'No,' admitted Orris. 'Probably not.'

He wasn't going to be allowed to sleep. Maybe he should wake up. With a great effort, Sylvan cracked open an eye. The faces were blurry. But they were definitely those of his brother and sister. At the sight of them a tiny warmth nestled in him. It was them. They were all right. He opened his other eye.

'Howz?' he said.

'Sylvan?' said Orris. 'Is that you?'

'Oh, for Sinethis's sake,' said Aven, shouldering Orris out of the way. 'Are you all right, Sylvan?'

Good question. Sylvan blinked a few times, trying to clear his head. He had a go at moving his legs. They responded stiffly, but the muscles flexed.

'Think so.'

'Can you stand?'

It took several attempts to roll to his feet, each accompanied by an agonizing cacophony of muscle cramps, but he managed it. His legs trembled, threatening to give way. He shoved them straight.

'Looks like it,' he said, slowly. 'Not sure about walking.'

Aven looked at his battered body. 'You look terrible,' she said.

'Thanks.'

Aven frowned. 'Where's Fern?'

The warmth was extinguished. A hollow feeling began to twist in Sylvan's gut. No. Not Fern. He closed his eyes.

'She's not here.' It was not a question.

'No. We haven't seen her since you left. We thought you were together.'

Sylvan squeezed his eyes tight. It wasn't fair. She should be here. It wasn't fair.

'Where is she, Sylvan? Where's Fern?' asked Aven, a note of panic in her voice.

But Sylvan could not answer. He had endured too much and hoped too hard. He had hoped that Fern had got back here, that they would all be waiting, that they would spend the night together as they always had. It had almost seemed possible.

Tears flowed helplessly down his cheeks and his breath came in thick sobs.

'I see,' said Aven quietly. She blinked rapidly, looking at the sky. She took a shaky breath. Then she said, 'Orris, help me, will you? We need to bring Sylvan home.'

The hollowness overtook him. He curled up. And somewhere, as if it were happening to somebody else and far, far beyond his control, two warm bodies nestled against his. He felt himself gently, but firmly, pushed to his feet. And somehow, his legs began to move beneath him. They pressed in close, holding him upright, lending him their strength.

Sylvan's sister and brother carried him, with the utmost care, back to the shelter of their tree. There, finally, the blissful darkness came up and took him.

Somewhere overhead a small bird sang. It flitted from its branch and skimmed across the Great River. It alighted in another tree. Sylvan, half hidden among the reeds of the feeding patch, watched it go. Around that patch the trees marched up and down the length of the Great River. This was not a place for River Singers, he thought. Perhaps it had been at one time, but then the trees had grown up and the grasses died. Or perhaps not. But downflow, and away from the Great River, were Singers who had never seen a mink, Singers who lived in a huge expanse of grass and water. He envied them. They were what he had hoped to find. But now the price for his hope seemed too high.

Sylvan stretched out his legs, the muscles still stiff from the previous day's struggles. He groomed his whiskers, as if the act could take away the loss. He was glad to be alone. Aven and Orris were dealing with things in their own way. They had stayed in the tree where it was safer. Sylvan had needed to come out, to find space to think. Now he was here, though, he could not focus, his mind instead turning restlessly over half-considered thoughts. He stared into Sinethis's depths. Even after everything he had been through he could still feel her urging him onward, driving him downflow. He hated that feeling. If he could he would have plucked it from him. Why should he follow? What good had it done him? What good were her tests, her warnings, her exhortations to be strong? He had been as strong as he could be, and still Fern was gone. He had been so sure that if he followed Sinethis she would keep them safe. But she hadn't. She had betrayed him.

A small rustle in the undergrowth behind him made him start, but then Fodur's slender features emerged from between the reeds.

'Ah. Thinks to find you here. Is OK to be joining you?'

Sylvan wanted desperately to be alone. Or perhaps he didn't. He heard himself say, 'Of course, Fodur.'

The rat limped forwards, moving with surprising speed on his three good legs. He held his injured hind leg curled up beneath him. When he was close enough Fodur sat awkwardly down next to Sylvan.

'You finds new place, then? Safe place for Singers? Know-nothing ratlings good for something, seems.'

'Yes, I found somewhere. It's not far away.'

'Is good then? Is safe.'

'We're not there yet,' said Sylvan sharply. Fodur flinched. Sylvan was instantly ashamed. None of this was Fodur's fault.

'I'm sorry,' said Sylvan. 'Yes, it's a good place. And it's thanks to you that I knew where to look. We owe you a lot.'

'Ack,' said Fodur. 'I says to you that nothing be owing between friends.'

'Still. Your leg . . . '

Fodur glanced back at it and then he grinned at Sylvan. 'Has been better, yes? But Fodur old rat. Has seen much. Has three more legs. Fodur has spares.' But then a serious look passed over Fodur's face. 'We all hurt, though, methinks. Is different, but same. I hears about Fern. Sorry I is. Is hard to lose, this I know.'

At Fern's name Sylvan stiffened. He really didn't want to talk about it; it was too soon. But Fodur, too, had lost family, once upon a time. And now, because of them, he was injured. The old rat had suffered much in his life, and if anyone had earned the right to speak of these things, he had. So instead of changing the subject Sylvan said, 'Yes, it's hard.'

Fodur did not reply, but simply sat companionably by

Sylvan's side. Sylvan looked down at the feeding sign lying at his feet, then back at the water. Words came to him, ones he could not speak to Orris or Aven. They trusted him too much. He still needed to be strong for them. But somehow he felt that he could tell Fodur.

'I got it wrong,' said Sylvan at last. 'I followed Sinethis, thinking she'd keep us safe. And now Fern's gone. This is all my fault.'

The rat said nothing for a long time. Then he said, 'Sinethis. Great River, yes?'

'Yes. The Great River.'

'We rats not have a Sinethis. She not speak with us. To us a river is a river.'

It had never occurred to Sylvan that the rats might not follow Sinethis. She had always just been there, as unquestionable as the soil and the sun. But it made sense, he supposed. Why would the rats follow her? They did not need her.

'So you have nothing to follow?'

'Ah,' said Fodur, with a slight chuckle. 'Is wrong that. We rats has many, many. We has Trickster and Mother, Hunter and Taker. These good things for rats. Is rat way. Sometime mayhaps we speaks with them, and mayhaps they guide. But is not always right to trust them. They's tricksy.' Fodur flexed his injured rear leg, wincing. 'Sees? Tricksy. You speak with

Sinethis, you follow?'

'Yes.'

'She leads to where she promises?'

Sylvan nodded. 'Yes. Mostly.'

'So this is good. Is right for Singers. We rats speak with others. Sometimes they keeps their promises. Is right for rats. And minks, too, mayhaps they speaks with more others. Mayhaps all of us has someone. But life is big. None of those we speak with promises we will live for ever. All of us will know how it is to lose. And is hard. I knows this and you knows this. But is not fault of Sylvan, Sinethis, or Fodur. Is not fault of anything. Is part of world. But so is rain, beetles, grasses. So is friends.'

The sun broke through trees and for a moment their little patch was bathed in warmth, filtered golden green by the reeds. Sylvan closed his eyes. Fern's loss was an empty, cold ache, still fresh. But somehow Fodur had helped a little. Perhaps there was still room for other things than grief. They sat for a moment, together in the reeds, enjoying the warmth.

'I think that we'll set off for the marsh tomorrow,' said Sylvan, slowly.

'I hears. Orris says so.'

'Will you come with us? It's a Singer place and I don't know how they'll take to having a rat around. But then Singers never really get along with each other anyway. I think we can find you a home.'

Fodur nodded. He smiled.

'Was hoping,' he said. 'Fodur needs home. And he like Singers. And Fodur good rat, thinks.'

Despite everything, Sylvan found himself smiling back. There was something infectious in Fodur's straightforward optimism.

'Yes. Fodur's a good rat,' he said. 'We'll be happy to have you with us. It'll probably mean trouble, but that's nothing new for us.'

'True. Fodur good at trouble.'

Sylvan stood up. 'Well, we'd better go and tell the others. There's a new home waiting for us, and in any case we can't stay here much longer. There's not much for Singers, here.'

Fodur stood and put a paw on Sylvan's shoulder. Then he limped back towards the hollow tree. Sylvan lingered for a few moments. He gazed over at Sinethis, flowing briskly past their little shelter; Sinethis who he had followed, fought, and cursed. Sinethis who had shown him the way. Is it true, he wondered, that she was just one among uncountable others? He shook his head. It didn't really matter, anyway. It wasn't as if he had any choice but to follow. He was a River Singer, and this was what he must do. At the thought, and just for a moment, the sound of the Great River swelled in him, her music in his mind. Then she withdrew, leaving the familiar ghost of warmth, urging him back downflow.

OK, OK, he thought. *We're going.*

He turned and began picking his way stiffly back to the tree. He was happy that Fodur would be going with them. There was still a long way to go before they were safe, and he had no idea how the other Singers would react to having a giant rat living among them. But it felt like the right thing to do. They would try to make it work. He thought back to his encounter with Camilla and Mistress Marjoram, and how disapproving Mistress Marjoram had been of him. If she felt like that about a single, hungry River Singer, he thought, just wait until she met his friends.

'Mother!'

Camilla's excited squeak cut through the drowsy hum of the insects. Mistress Marjoram sighed and stood up out of the pleasant shade in which she had been feeding. A day's respite, she reflected, was probably too much to ask.

'What is it?'

'It's him, Mother,' said Camilla. 'He's back.'

'What "him"? What are you talking about?'

'Sylvan. He's come back.'

Sylvan. Mistress Marjoram searched her memory for the name. What she found there did not please her.

'You mean the vagabond idiot?'

'Yes, Mother,' Camilla sighed. 'Anyway, he's down at the bottom of the territory. He says he would like your permission to pass through with his family.'

'Oh, would he now? Well we'll see about that. I'm not about to allow a troupe of vagabonds to march through here. That's quite out of the question.'

Mistress Marjoram set off, trailing Camilla in her wake.

'Mother, he's not really a vagabond.'

'I know a vagabond when I see one, and that young vole was a vagabond through and through. Don't contradict me.'

Mistress Marjoram marched down to the trees at the downflow extent of her territory until she spotted the Sylvan male. He was sitting impudently in what was left of the iris he had destroyed on his last visit. As she approached he straightened.

'Good morning, Mistress Marjoram,' he said. 'It's a pleasure to see you.'

Mistress Marjoram fixed him with a suspicious stare. He did not sound quite like the same vole. He looked different too; a bit better groomed, perhaps, and not so dazed.

'Is it? And why would that be? Hungry again, are you?' she said, attempting a cold archness. She was rather pleased with the effect, but it seemed not to register.

'No, thank you. We found a nice patch of sedges back in the woods and we fed there. We didn't want to impose.'

'And who might "we" be, exactly?'

'I told you, Mother,' said Camilla from behind her, 'Sylvan has family with him.'

'That's right,' said Sylvan. 'Four of us. My brother and sister and our friend, Fodur. We were wondering if it would be all right to pass through your territory? We wouldn't bother you, but it seems to be the only way into the marsh.'

'Ah. So you're heading to the marsh, are you?' asked Mistress Marjoram, giving her daughter an I-told-you-so look. 'Well, I'm certain you'll fit right in there.'

'There's plenty of space there,' Camilla chipped in. 'I'd like to go there myself one day, except—'

'Except that it's not a suitable place for a well bred young vole like her,' said Mistress Marjoram. 'You have your family with you, you say? Let's have a look at them, then.'

Sylvan called back into the edge of the wood and a couple more young voles came forward, stopping beside him. One was a male, as big as any full grown Singer she had seen. He was a bit glum, though, and kept his eyes on the ground. The other was a small female. She had a feisty air about her that Mistress Marjoram instinctively disliked. The female stared right back at her, impudently.

'You said there were four of you,' pointed out Mistress Marjoram.

'Yes,' said Sylvan with an odd look. 'But Fodur's very shy. He'd prefer not to be seen.'

'Nonsense. I'm not going to give anyone permission to pass through here unless I've met them personally.'

'I really don't think—' Sylvan began.

'I don't care what you think. This is my territory and I demand to meet your friend.'

Sylvan shrugged. 'OK,' he said. 'If that's what you want. Fodur, could you please come and meet Mistress Marjoram?'

Mistress Marjoram was not quite sure what happened next. Later, when she had recovered, she would tell anyone who would listen how she had met an appalling monster, quite hideous, with a horribly pointed face and which spoke a ghastly mishmash of the most coarse Singer's words imaginable. And then it attacked her, viciously. Yes. That was it. She was quite certain that it had attacked her. She knew that because everything had gone black and, when she awoke, it, and the rest of that vagabond's family, was gone. When she said these things, though, she felt a small unease and avoided Camilla's eye. But, she thought, this sort of thing was just typical of what happened if you let vagabonds into your territory.

The small group left Mistress Marjoram's tiny stretch of river behind them and set off upflow. Camilla, once they had calmed her down, had eventually been persuaded to give them directions to the marsh. She had seemed very reluctant to see them go, Aven commented, giving

Sylvan a sly look. Sylvan ignored her. They went carefully. After Mistress Marjoram's reaction to Fodur, Sylvan was taking no chances. It was best, he decided, to avoid contact with other Singers completely. Now if they heard a rustle they left the water and looped away into the fringing vegetation, avoiding the territory owners. It was slow going but at least they encountered no more bother.

After a small distance their path was intersected by a ditch. They took it, heading further into the fields towards the marsh proper. This far out, the signs of Singers were few, but as they walked the plants became thicker and greener and the waters more still and inviting. The few feeding signs they saw were fresh and succulent.

Orris fell in alongside Sylvan. 'What do you think?' he asked, nodding at the swathes of grass.

'What? Oh, yes. It looks OK, I suppose.'

'Funny that Mistress Marjoram fainting like that. I thought she was going to give us trouble until then.'

'Yeah, funny,' said Sylvan, distractedly.

'Fodur was quite offended.'

'Was he? That's good.'

Orris gave him a look. 'All right, Sylvan. You're not listening. What's the matter?'

Sylvan cast a look back over his shoulder to where Fodur was limping alongside Aven.

'I didn't like the way that Mistress Marjoram reacted, that's all.'

'So she's ignorant. So were we.'

'I still don't like it.'

'Come on, Sylvan. It's not like you to be this gloomy. I know it's been hard. It's been horrible for all of us. And I miss Fern. But we're nearly there.'

Sylvan smiled in reply, but it felt strained. 'I'm sorry. It's just . . . Oh, I don't know. Something doesn't feel right. I won't be happy until we're settled. Too many things could go wrong.'

Orris put his head on one side. 'You know what I think? I think we only made it this far because you kept going no matter what. You didn't think about what could go wrong, you just did what you had to.'

'You're right,' said Sylvan, bitterly. 'I didn't think before I did things. I just took risks. Fern always said that. And now she's gone. It's my fault.'

Orris stopped dead. He put a paw on Sylvan and turned him to face him. 'What are you talking about? Of course you took risks. As you said: everything we do is a risk. That's just the way River Singers are. I didn't understand it before, but now I do. And it was you that told me. Don't lose that. Not now.'

Sylvan could not think of a reply. He was spared having to respond by Aven and Fodur stopping beside them. Fodur surveyed the screen of grasses between them and the open sky. He flicked an ear.

'Is cosy this, yes? But thinks it better for Singers to be further in marsh.'

'What he means is, "get a move on",' said Aven.

'We were waiting for you, hairy face,' said Sylvan, vaguely. 'But you've got a point, Fodur. Let's keep going.'

Aven cast an eye skyward. Against the blue, a black shape circled. 'What's that?'

'Ah. I has seen it. Is harrier, methinks. Dangerous birdie.'

'Dangerous?' asked Orris, nervously.

'For froggies. Eats them. Not so bad for Singers.'

The water voles stared at him.

'Is rat joke,' Fodur clarified. 'Is fun, fun, yes?'

'Hilarious,' said Aven. The distant shape drifted across the sun and a bird call sounded across the marsh. 'Just in case it's short-sighted and can't tell the difference between a frog and a vole, don't you think we'd better get going?'

Sylvan led the way. Their ditch intersected with another, and then another, leading them further into the Wetted Land. The Singers' signs grew more frequent. Time and again they looped away from the water to avoid a resident. And time and again a brief inspection of the boundary marks showed that both territories to each side were occupied. After a detour through a small patch of woodland to avoid what sounded like a particularly big female, Sylvan was beginning to doubt whether they would ever find anywhere. But even as he opened his mouth to say so, Aven gave an excited squeak.

'Sylvan. Come and look at this.'

Sylvan was quickly at her side. She was sitting next to a River Singer's marker, looking pleased with herself. Sylvan inspected it. It looked like any other pile of droppings. He gave it an experimental sniff. It smelt like a female Singer. That was all he could tell.

'Right,' said Sylvan. 'It's a boundary mark. What's so exciting?'

'Can't you smell it?'

'I don't smell markers. Why don't you just assume I'm an idiot and answer the question?'

'Fair enough. What's so exciting, idiot, is that there's only one female's scent here. And she's back that way.' Aven gestured back along the ditch, the way they had come. 'There's no female in the territory ahead. We might have found somewhere.'

Sylvan peered down the ditch ahead of them. It looked like a Singer's dream. The water was deep, clear, and still, and the grasses and sedges were tall and lush.

'Aven,' he said, 'are you absolutely sure?'

Aven gave it another sniff, and nodded. 'Really,' she said. 'There's definitely no other female. In fact, watch this.'

Aven went to the marker and deposited some droppings of her own and spent some moments scraping scent onto them. She adjusted it for a while and then turned back to the others, grinning.

'I've been wanting to do that for *ages*,' she said. She sniffed at the marker. 'Much better.' But then she frowned. 'You know, I can smell a couple of different males here, though. They might cause problems.'

THE WETTED LAND

Sylvan glanced back at Orris. He didn't know how the resident males would react to having a couple of new males around. They probably wouldn't greet them with open paws, though.

'It could, yes. But I suppose we'll deal with that when we come to it. OK. It sounds like we might have found somewhere, but I want to be certain before we get too settled. Let's go the whole length. Aven, you go first and let me know if your amazing dropping-smelling abilities tell you anything interesting.'

She aimed a cuff at him, which he dodged, and set off along the bank. Despite his earlier pessimism, his spirits were beginning to lift. Could it be true? Could they have found their new home? He was impatient to get to the far end, to see if there really was no female living here. He followed Aven, with Orris and Fodur right behind him. It became more and more clear that the territory was empty. The few droppings on the banks belonged to males. And it was a big length of ditch: bigger by far than Mistress Marjoram's place, and even larger than their mother's territory had been. It seemed an incredibly long time before Aven called back to them.

'It's here. It's the edge of the territory. I can smell the next female.'

'That's great,' said Sylvan. 'Why don't you get back here and we'll make a plan?'

'Hang on. I'll be back in a bit. Just got some marking to do.'

'She's obsessed,' said Sylvan.

'Is natural,' commented Fodur. 'Is good for Singers. Not want to be fighting other females.'

Orris was staring about him looking stunned. 'It's a territory. And it's all empty,' he said.

'It's not quite empty,' said Sylvan. 'It's got an Aven in it now. And I don't think she'll be giving it up easily.'

Sylvan looked around. A tree was set back a little from the ditch. Along the bank were several large examples of the tussocks that Mistress Marjoram had mentioned. Grasses and reeds grew from the water and hustled thickly on the bank edges. He could smell no predators and the bird calls were friendly. He had to admit that it looked good. But still he could not shake the feeling that something was amiss. Even here in Sinethis's sleepy backwaters, he could not believe that she did not have more in store for them, one final test.

Aven pattered into view, grinning happily. 'That should do it. Fresh scent. It'll give the other females something to think about. We might have got somewhere,' she said.

Sylvan smiled back, wearily. 'That's great. Really. But we're going to have to be careful and take things easy. There's no way of knowing what else might be in this territory. Let's not take any risks.'

Aven gave him an odd look. 'Are you feeling all right?'

'I wish everyone would stop asking me that.'

'Well are you?'

'No, I'm not, because you all keep asking me stupid questions. Look. I don't know about anybody else but I'm getting hungry. It really does look like this place might be empty, and I know that you've decided it's yours, Aven, but it's still unfamiliar and there's almost certainly going to be more work to do. We'll be better prepared on full stomachs, so let's have some food and then we can explore properly.'

The others needed no encouragement. Within moments they were tucking into the vegetation. Fodur stood aside, surveying the plants with a disappointed air.

'You all right, Fodur?' asked Sylvan between mouthfuls.

'Am, yes, Sylvan. But here not good rat food. Mayhaps I has a little explore while you's eating?'

Sylvan nodded. 'OK. Be careful though.'

Fodur smiled. 'This your place, now. Rats is OK here, methinks.'

Sylvan watched Fodur limp off back along the bank, pausing to

sniff at a clump of blue forget-me-nots. He smiled. Then he turned back to his food.

Peaceful moments rolled by. Orris and Aven moved down the bank, grazing a little distance apart. The sun was warm, and the sound of the slow-moving water, so unlike the swift flow of Sinethis they had grown up with, was lulling. They saw no sign of any other vole. Sylvan dared to hope that this was it, that they had made it.

'Sylvan! Singers!'

Sylvan's head snapped up. Down the bank Aven and Orris also came alert. It had been Fodur's voice, strained and urgent. Sylvan threw down his grass and sprinted, overtaking the others. They fell in behind him, dashing downstream, jumping roots, splashing through shallows. Sylvan crashed through a final stand of reeds and skidded to a stop in a small clear space on the bank. Orris came to a stop behind him, shortly followed by Aven. In the centre of the clearing was Fodur, hunched in on himself, head curled beneath his body, forepaws protectively over his ears.

THE WETTED LAND

He was bleeding from a small bite wound At their approach two River Singers stepped away from Fodur, watching the new arrivals warily. Sylvan sized them up. They were both males. The bigger of the two had a scar across his face, and exuded confidence. The other already had one eye on the vegetation, as if planning an escape.

Things were looking bad, Sylvan thought. The males had attacked Fodur, and probably would have tried to kill him had they not been interrupted. But even as Sylvan surveyed the scene, he felt his heart growing oddly light. The indefinable dread he had carried for the last days vanished. The Great River lapped within him, filling him with a quiet determination.

This was it, he realized. This was Sinethis's final challenge. This is what he had been worrying about. Sylvan eyed the males. They were larger than he was and the same size as Orris. That could cause trouble. But Sylvan had fought a mink and survived. He had escaped from a fox and a pack of rats and battled Sinethis's rapids. He had led his family down the length of the Great River to find a new home. There was no way that a couple of male Singers were going to spoil things now.

'Fodur, are you OK?' he called.

'No I isn't,' came Fodur's indignant response, muffled by his belly fur. 'They attacks me.'

It was obvious that Fodur wasn't badly hurt. Sylvan weighed his options. He did not want a fight, but with Fodur, Aven, and Orris, the other males were outnumbered. The odds were with them. Still, there was something in the scar-faced vole's expression that he didn't like. He looked as if he might enjoy making trouble. Sylvan thought fast. There must be a way of defusing this. Something like what Fodur did back with those juvenile rats . . .

'OK, Fodur,' he called. 'Don't worry. We'll sort this out.'

Sylvan turned to Orris and Aven and motioned at them to stay where they were. Then he walked towards the males until he stood a little in front of Fodur, between them and the rat.

'Good afternoon,' he said, cheerfully. 'What seems to be the problem?'

The males looked at each other and back at Sylvan.

'What?' said Scar-face.

'I asked if there was a problem,' said Sylvan, pleasantly.

Scar-face gestured at Fodur. 'Yeah. There is. That's the problem.'

'Really?' Sylvan feigned surprise. 'I wouldn't have thought Fodur would cause a problem. You weren't causing any problems, were you, Fodur?'

'May have, methinks, or wouldn't be bleeding.'

'That's one way of looking at it. Did he really cause a problem?' Sylvan asked.

'What are you talking about?' said Scar-face. 'He's a rat, isn't he?'

'Is he?' Sylvan turned back to Fodur. 'Are you really a rat, Fodur?'

'Yes, I's a rat,' came the muffled confirmation, followed by muttering which sounded very like, 'now stops mucking about and help me.'

Sylvan turned to his brother and sister. 'Did you know about this?'

Orris stared as if Sylvan had gone insane. Thankfully, Aven understood. She stepped forward and stood beside Sylvan. There were now two water voles between Fodur and the males.

'Now you mention it, I had my suspicions. There *was* something odd about his ears. I just thought he was deformed, poor love. That and the terrible speech impediment and the bald tail. Not pretty, I admit—'

'Thanks you.'

'—but I never would have guessed he's a rat.'

'Oh. Oh well, so there you have it,' said Sylvan to the males, who were looking bewildered. 'Looks like he might be a rat.' He shrugged.

The males looked uncomfortable. Sylvan let the silence grow.

The smaller male cleared his throat. 'Rats eat Singers' pups. They steal our burrows. They're not to be trusted.'

'Do you do that, Fodur?'

Fodur's muffled response was barely discernible.

'What'd he say?' asked Scar-face, suspiciously.

'He said he wouldn't because they'd taste bad.'

The males looked even more uncertain now. Attacking a potentially vicious enemy was one thing, but it was difficult to attack a reasonable-sounding rodent like Fodur, especially if they would have to fight past two River Singers to get to him. *We might*, Sylvan thought, *just about get away with this.*

Given even a little more time the males might have lost interest, decided it was too much bother, and gone on their way. But at that moment the female from the next territory ran out of the reeds into the clearing and stopped dead. Her eyes fixed on Aven, with an unfriendly glint. Aven returned it, coolly.

'I heard voices,' said the newcomer. 'And smelt a new female's scent on my boundary. I thought that I'd come and get acquainted. Just wanted to make sure that we all know where our limits lie. We wouldn't want any disagreements, would we.' She looked Aven up and down. 'Especially if we're small.'

Sylvan winced. Aven smiled, showing more of her teeth than was strictly necessary. She advanced until she was nose to nose with the other female.

'Hello,' she said, sweetly. 'My name is Aven. What's yours?'

'Lily. A pleasure.' Her tone suggested otherwise.

'Well, Lily, we're going to be neighbours. As you pointed out, I am quite small. But I'm also exceptionally vicious. I've got a horrible temper and when I bite I make sure that I do it right where it counts. And I don't let go. Ever. So, do you think we should be friends?'

Whatever Mistress Lily had been expecting, it probably was not Aven. Mistress Lily nodded, taken aback. Aven continued, still in the same sweetly reasonable tone, 'That's good, because I don't like biting females. I only do it if they call me "small". But you're my friend now. And that's a good thing. Now, why don't we, as friends, go and have a look at that boundary marker? And while we're there we can discuss our limits.'

Aven began to escort the stunned-looking Mistress Lily off her territory. That should have been the end of it, but just before they reached the reeds Mistress Lily happened to glance back. She caught sight of Fodur's still-huddled form and her eyes widened. She stopped dead and gave a tiny scream.

'What is that?' she demanded, pointing at Fodur with a quivering paw.

Nobody spoke.

'I asked a question,' said Mistress Lily, her voice shrill. 'I must be answered. What is it?'

Scar-face looked from Sylvan to Orris. Then he gave a sly smile.

'It's a rat, Mistress Lily,' he said.

Mistress Lily had hysterics.

'It's a rat,' she shrieked. 'It's a rat and it's going to eat my babies! Somebody do something about it! Get rid of it, immediately.'

Aven grabbed Mistress Lily and bundled her out of the clearing, ushering her firmly back to her own territory. But even as they disappeared from view, Sylvan could see that the damage was done. A nasty smile had spread across Scar-face's features.

'Well, well. You heard Mistress Lily,' he said. 'Rats are no good. Me and my colleague here are going to have to deal with this one. You'd be advised to step aside.'

'Come on—' Sylvan began, but the other male, emboldened by Scar-face's words, advanced on him.

'Get out of the way.'

'I'm not in your way,' said Sylvan, desperately. The two males muscled forwards, forcing Sylvan to take a step back.

'The rat, my friend, is not welcome,' said Scar-face. 'Mistress Lily don't like rats and we don't like things that upset Mistress Lily.' He gestured at Sylvan and Orris. 'You two are Singers. Fair enough. You can find yourselves a place. But the rat is going.'

'Yeah, we'll deal with it. Don't you worry,' said the smaller male, grinning unpleasantly.

Sylvan was running out of options. There was no way he could win in a fight against two males. But he would not abandon Fodur. He tensed.

'No!'

The sound came from Orris. His normally placid face was contorted with rage. He stalked forwards until he was standing next to Sylvan, facing the males.

'Fodur is our friend. This is our sister's territory. Fodur stays. You go.'

Sylvan gave Orris a look of pure disbelief. 'Orris . . . ' he began.

'I'm not having it,' Orris shouted. 'I let Fodur get hurt once, but not this time. They think they can attack him

just because he's injured. But if they want to hurt him, they'll have to fight me first.'

Scar-face turned to the other male. 'Big words, those. I wonder if he's up to them.'

There was no other warning. Scar-face launched at Orris, teeth bared. And then they were rolling over and over, squeaking, clawing, and biting. Orris got his legs between him and Scar-face, and shoved, throwing the other vole off. The male rolled to his feet and flung himself at Orris once more. Orris went over backwards, borne to the ground by the ferocity of the attack. But in an instant he had twisted free and his teeth snapped at Scar-face's neck, making him jerk away. The two River Singers broke apart and circled, breathing hard. Then they leapt, colliding in a flurry of blows, teeth and paws flashing and pummelling. They toppled over, still locked together, and rolled down the bank into the water. Even in the water they grappled, gasping and splashing.

Sylvan glanced at the smaller male who was watching the scene with fascination.

Sylvan was almost desperate to jump in, to help Orris. But if he did there was no telling what the other male might do. Even as Sylvan hesitated the two voles in the water broke apart. Orris swam three strokes away, and Sylvan thought that his brother had lost, that he was running. But then Orris turned and dived straight at the other, grabbing for his head and shoving him bodily beneath the surface. Scar-face gave a terrible gasp as both voles disappeared from view.

The waters closed over the two voles. Sylvan and the smaller male ran to the water's edge, looking for any sign of the combatants. There was none. Ripples expanded to the shoreline, lapping at the plants. Sylvan held his breath, watching the calm place in the water where seconds earlier Orris had been fighting. No sign of either vole. Bubbles rose to the surface and stopped. The waters became smooth, unbroken. Sylvan waited. Nothing. Orris and Scar-face were gone. The smaller male near to Sylvan made a movement and Sylvan whirled, up on his haunches, own teeth bared.

'Don't even think about it,' he shouted. 'Leave the rat alone or I'll chew your face off. This is our place now. You don't belong here.'

His companion gone, the other male backed nervously away. 'All right,' he said. 'No need to get violent.'

Sylvan advanced.

'What?' he yelled. '*What*?' He gestured at the still surface of the water. 'My brother is down there because of you. He's gone. Orris is gone. This is all your fault. I'm going to kill you.'

Fodur uncurled with amazing speed and placed himself between Sylvan and the other male. Poised to attack, Sylvan fell awkwardly forward onto his feet.

'Get out of my way, Fodur.'

'Sylvan, no. Not good for Singers. Let him be.'

'Get out of my way. I'm going to hurt him.'

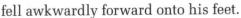

The rat shook his head, 'Not good idea, methinks.'

Sylvan tried to run round Fodur but the rat blocked his path. The small male shrank back further.

Sylvan's voice was a low hiss. 'Move, Fodur, or I'll—'

'What, Sylvan? Fight Fodur? For what?'

Fodur looked crestfallen. He dropped his gaze but

remained between Sylvan and the other vole. Sylvan stood, chest heaving, glaring at the rat and the vole behind him. Then, slowly, he took a step back.

'No. Of course not. You're right. I'm sorry, Fodur.'

'Is OK. Fodur understand.'

'But we still need to do something about this.' Sylvan gestured at the male. 'I'm not having him go away and cause more problems.'

'Mayhaps best if Fodur have talks with him.'

Fodur limped over to the male vole and regarded him solemnly. The male looked as though it would rather be anywhere else.

'So,' said Fodur, companionably. 'I's a rat, yes?'

'Yes,' said the male.

'Is good. And you's a Singer. Is good. I takes it you not have problems with rats no more?'

The male stared past Fodur at the savage expression on Sylvan's face. He shook his head fervently. 'No, not me.'

'Is good.' Fodur leaned forwards. The male stepped back. 'And methinks that you'll be telling your friends that I's OK: nice ratty, to be left in peace. Eh?'

The male nodded.

'And the other rat-friend Singers here? They's to be left alone?'

More nodding.

'Good. Tells you what, then: I give you no troubles, you does me no harm, everyone happy. Yes?'

Nodding.

'Nice Singer.' Fodur pressed forwards until their noses almost touched. 'Now go away.'

The male fled. Sylvan walked to the water's edge. It looked as though nothing had even so much as rippled the surface. No sign of Orris. He stared numbly at it. Fodur joined him.

'I's sorry, Sylvan. I causes troubles. Thinks I should not have come.'

Sylvan shook his head, not taking his eyes off the water. 'It's not your fault, Fodur. You have as much right to be here as anyone. It's those stupid, ignorant . . . '

Sylvan could find no more words. He closed his eyes. Fodur moved closer to his friend. When Aven returned from escorting Mistress Lily back to her territory she found Sylvan huddled at the water's edge with an unusually silent Fodur sitting beside him.

'Oh good, those males are gone then,' said Aven. 'Where's Orris?'

Neither Sylvan or Fodur answered.

'Where is he?' demanded Aven.

Fodur raised his head. 'He fight male in water. They not come back. I's sorry.'

'Oh.'

Aven slumped to the ground beside them. They sat in silence while Sinethis lapped at the sweet-grass shore. They listened to her sounds: the birds and the insects and the susurration of the reeds. They gazed at the water and wondered how this could have happened, now, when they had finally thought they were safe.

A slight rustle.

'What on earth are you all looking at?'

The voice sounded grumpy. Sylvan spun round and his mouth dropped open. Aven too was gaping. It was Orris: wet, scratched, and dishevelled, but otherwise intact.

'What's the problem?' said Orris.

Sylvan's mouth opened and closed a few times but no sounds emerged.

'Well, you might look a bit happier. It's not like I've just had a fight or anything.'

'Is Orris. Is OK,' said Fodur, happily.

'Well, I'm not, really,' said Orris, 'I'm—'

He got no further before Aven flung herself on him. Sylvan was close behind her. He went down under the weight of a pair of jubilant water voles. Then Sylvan pulled away.

'Where have you been?' he demanded. 'What happened to the other Singer?'

'I don't think we'll be seeing him again,' said Orris. 'Once I shoved him under, he dived to the bottom and tried to swim for it. So I chased him. We swam all the way down to the next territory and I bit him when he tried to climb out. I've never heard anything squeak like that.'

'Amazing,' said Sylvan, shaking his head.

A sheepish smile spread across Orris's face. 'So I did OK, then?'

'More than,' said Sylvan. 'You did brilliantly.'

'Orris, I'm so proud of you,' said Aven. For a moment Orris's smile widened. Then he coughed and busied himself with grooming.

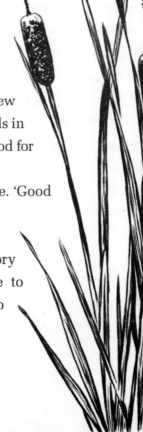

Fodur stood a little distance apart, watching with a smile. Sylvan went over to him.

'So. It looks like this is our new home,' said Sylvan, testing the words in his mouth. 'What do you think? Good for rats?'

Fodur put his head on one side. 'Good for rats,' he said.

'I'm glad,' said Sylvan.

'Of course, this is my territory now,' said Aven. 'So you'll have to behave yourselves if you want to stay. I bite, you know.'

He smiled at his sister. 'Whatever you say, Tiny.'

'Don't call me that.'

Sylvan grinned. Orris surveyed the ditch and the plants. He gave an approving nod.

'It's nice,' he said. 'I think I'll like it here.'

Sylvan blinked. Orris really did sound like a different vole.

'But I could do with somewhere to sleep.'

Ah. Of course. Sylvan supposed that some things might take longer to change than others.

'Well,' said Sylvan, 'I suppose we'll have to see if there are any burrows. I might go have a look at some of those tussocks. They could do the job. Any of you fancy having a look around?'

'I'll go that way,' said Orris gesturing up along the ditch. 'I could do with a bit of an explore. Coming, Fodur?'

'Is plan, that. Fodur still needs to eat.'

The pair of them walked off, quickly hidden by the plants.

'I might go and reinforce some markers,' said Aven. 'I have a territory now, don't you know.'

'Really?' said Sylvan. 'I hadn't noticed.'

'It's a serious responsibility, being horrible to all those other females,' Aven said. 'And I'm going to be *good* at it.'

She gave him a nudge and headed off down towards Mistress Lily's territory. Sylvan watched her go, almost pitying Mistress Lily. Alone, now, fatigue washed through him. And with the fatigue was something else; the absence of something. Now everything was done he felt a curious hollowness inside. For as long as he could remember he had been following Sinethis, heading downstream, following an urge deep in his breast. And now the urge had disappeared. They had arrived and Sinethis was finally finished with him. The feeling had gone. The journey was over.

Sylvan took a deep breath and let it go. He gazed around him. *Home*, he thought. *Home*. It had come at a heavy price. He wished more than anything that Fern was here with them, safe in a new colony. But Fern was gone, and there was nothing he could do. He put the thoughts from his mind. There would be time to grieve later, but now there were things to be done. There were burrows to find and preparations to be made for the night. He stood on legs wearied from long travels and, with a sniff of the air, followed in the direction that Aven had gone. They still had a home to build. He would not rest until it was done.

The dawn was bright and the waters quiet. Sylvan awoke. He yawned. He opened his eyes. He smiled, softly. Today was a new day.

Just beyond the entrance to his tussock-burrow was a place where the iris was thick and juicy. He was hungry. He pattered down from his nest and out into the chill morning air. This early the sun was weak, but it cast long shadows, perfect to hide a feeding Singer. As he ate he surveyed their home. The Great River did not flow here. These were her back waters, her forgotten places, a haven far from the rushing and pounding of her main flow. He was grateful for it. A few times, in the days since

they had arrived, he had tried to listen, to hear Sinethis's song in the stillness. But she did not come to him. The few snatches he had caught held deep, slow notes, speaking of warm contentment and long days. Gone was the discord, left far behind. Sylvan was not fooled, though. There were still enemies in this marsh; the fox, heron, stoat. The bargain was the same, even here. Sinethis offered protection but still each day was one in which he could be taken. He understood, now, of sacrifice and of Sinethis. He knew her songs: the gentle ones that make it good to be alive and the hard ones that you must fight with everything you have. He had earned his respite, but she may yet have more for him to do. And if she called he must follow. That too was part of the bargain. The memory of his mother's words, so long ago now, echoed in his mind.

She sings with us a song as soft as thistles, hard as roots, deep as shadows, old as stones. We sing with her a song as quick as thinking, sweet as apples, brief as day. We are River Singers and we are hers.

THE RIVER SINGERS

Our songs are short, Sylvan thought, *so we must sing them well.* He munched the iris, savouring its sweetness. The song here, he had to admit, could be a lot worse. When he was finished he left the feeding sign in a pile as a Singer should, and picked a direction. There was a new world here, ready to be explored by an inquisitive water vole. He rose onto his haunches and scented the breeze. It was fresh and cool. No enemies. Not yet. Somewhere above him the marsh harrier called, but it was far away. He dropped to his feet and began threading his way through the grasses. This was his world. It was every bit as wonderful as he had once dreamed it would be. It was also immeasurably more terrible. It was his, though. And it was just as it should be.

The story will continue in

THE RISING

Coming Soon . . .

Tom Moorhouse lives in Oxford.
When not writing fiction he works
as an ecologist at Oxford University's
Zoology Department. Over the years
he has met quite a lot of wildlife.
Most of it tried to bite him. He loves
hiking up mountains, walking through
woods, climbing on rocks, and generally
being weather-beaten outdoors.
THE RIVER SINGERS is his first novel.